"I got it!" Aidan cried. "You and Dad can get married.

"Then we can all move into the new house when it's put together. Like a family."

Natalie's gaze drifted across the road. "I wish it could be that simple, A, but it's not."

"Why?"

Natalie shot Evan a pleading look.

"Hey, buddy. Sometimes moms and dads live together and sometimes they don't. Even though we don't live together, that doesn't change how we feel about you."

"But I want us to be a family with one house, not two."

Truth be told, at one time, Evan had wanted the same thing.

But things were different now.

He and Nat were different.

He wanted a wife who could trust him with her deepest fears and secrets—with her whole heart.

And that wasn't Natalie.

As much as Evan wanted to make his son's wish come true, there was too much to overcome before they all could be the family that Aidan wanted…

Heart, home and faith have always been important to **Lisa Jordan**, so writing stories with those elements comes naturally. Happily married for over thirty years to her real-life hero, she and her husband have two grown sons, and they are embracing their new season of grandparenting. Lisa enjoys quality time with her family, reading good books and being creative with friends. Learn more about her and her writing by visiting www.lisajordanbooks.com.

Books by Lisa Jordan

Love Inspired

Lakeside Reunion
Lakeside Family
Lakeside Sweethearts
Lakeside Redemption
Lakeside Romance
Season of Hope
A Love Redeemed
The Father He Deserves

Visit the Author Profile page at Harlequin.com.

The Father
He Deserves

Lisa Jordan

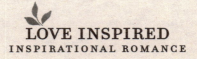

LOVE INSPIRED

INSPIRATIONAL ROMANCE

Recycling programs for this product may not exist in your area.

ISBN-13: 978-1-335-75865-1

The Father He Deserves

This edition published by arrangement with Harlequin Books S.A.

For questions and comments about the quality of this book, please contact us at CustomerService@Harlequin.com.

Love Inspired
22 Adelaide St. West, 40th Floor
Toronto, Ontario M5H 4E3, Canada
www.Harlequin.com

Printed in U.S.A.

Have not I commanded thee? Be strong and of a good courage; be not afraid, neither be thou dismayed: for the Lord thy God is with thee whithersoever thou goest.

—*Joshua* 1:9

To my family members and friends
who battle fear and anxiety on a daily basis.
I'm not naming you, but you know who you are.
You are warriors! Embrace His grace
to live your best life. I love you!

Acknowledgments

Thank you to Jeanne Takenaka, Tari Faris,
Mindy Obenhaus, Mandy Boerma,
Alena Tauriainen, Pennylynn Moga,
Carrie Padgett, Kathy Copen, Keli Gwyn,
Christina Myerly, Jamie Jo Wright and
Tonya LaCourse for brainstorming,
book research and beta reading.

Thanks to my MBT Core team, JOY Seekers,
Coffee Girls and WWC family—your prayers and
encouragement keep me going…and growing.
I love you all.

Thank you to my family—Patrick, Mitchell,
Scott, Sarah and Bridget. You are my strongest
cheerleaders and reasons for reaching for
my dreams. I love you forever.

Thanks to Rachelle Gardner and Melissa Endlich
for continually encouraging and inspiring me to
grow as a writer. So thankful you're on my team.
And to the Love Inspired team who works hard to
bring my books to print.

Finally, and most important, to Jesus, who
helps me to be brave so I can live my best life.

Chapter One

Evan hated returning home a failure.

He wanted nothing more than to hole up in his restored 1970s RV, dubbed the Water Wagon by his River Rats teammates, watch his favorite paddling channel on his laptop, and drown his sorrows with a dripping burger and greasy fries, but that wasn't the Holland way. Especially since he'd driven through the night to surprise his dad for his sixty-fifth birthday. Maybe with the early-evening backyard barbecue going on, he could dodge questions he had no desire to answer.

For a few hours, at least.

After coming up the back side of Holland Hill, Evan parked his RV on the other side of the barn, pocketed his keys and gave River, his rescued yellow Labrador retriever, an affectionate pat. "Ready to go to a party?"

River's tail thumped against the cushion on the passenger seat and he lifted his nose into Evan's hand. Evan exited the RV, rounded the front and opened the passenger door. After releasing River from his seat belt harness, he clipped a leash onto his collar and stepped back as the yellow Lab jumped to the ground. Evan turned and nearly whacked his elbow on the open door. His muscles tensed and pulled across his back. Muscles still recovering from the traumatic kayak flip and dunking that had jeopardized his paddling career.

"Come on, River. Let's go find Dad."

The Holland Family Farm sat atop Holland Hill on the outskirts of Shelby Lake in northwestern Pennsylvania. The early-August heat blanketed Evan. A breeze brushed his face, carrying the scent of freshly cut and rolled bales of hay drying in the fields.

Evan breathed deep.

As he passed along the barbed wire—fenced pasture, black-and-white cows eyed him, then returned to eating grass and swishing away flies with their tails. Rows of corn stood tall, ready for harvesting, the corn silk on the ears having turned from a gold to a dark brown.

"Knee high by the Fourth of July" had been the mantra for as long as he could remember.

Looked like it was going to be a good harvest this year.

The farm deserved it.

They strode past the barn, which still caused his insides to clench, and the cars and pickups lining both sides of the country road. He followed the music and laughter to the backyard.

Curls of smoke from the grill spiraled through the air, sending scents of seared meat straight to his gut.

His stomach rumbled.

When was the last time he'd eaten? Probably the Snickers bar he'd bought a couple of hours ago after crossing the state line and stopping for gas.

Rounding the corner of the farmhouse that had been

home for the first couple decades of his life, his focus zeroed in on locating a burger of some sort.

He collided with a soft body with enough of a jolt to his left arm—pinned in a surgical sling—that he sucked in a sharp breath. "Oof."

He dropped River's leash and shot out a hand to steady the person wearing a navy baseball hat and sunglasses. "Sorry. Are you okay?"

The person looked up. Despite the oversize frames shielding her eyes, he'd recognize that heart-shaped face in a lineup.

His heart shuddered to a stop.

"Nat." Her name wheezed out as his eyes widened.

Her dark brown hair had been pulled into a ponytail and looped through the back opening in her hat. She wore a pink T-shirt printed with the word *LOVE*, a paw print replacing the *O*. Her cuffed navy shorts exposed long legs.

Looking as gorgeous as ever.

She removed her sunglasses slowly and assessed him with those bottle-green eyes, hard as glass. "Evan."

She took in his rumpled olive T-shirt emblazoned with Go Big or Go Home—the irony not lost on him, faded jeans with a threadbare patch on the thigh and worn leather flip-flops. Maybe he should have changed into something more presentable. At least he'd had the foresight to get his mop chopped and shave the six-week growth from his face.

Her eyes settled on River, heeled at his side, her lips lifting into a smile. Then she shifted her attention to Evan's left arm, the smile giving way to a frown. "What happened?"

"Arthroscopic shoulder surgery."

"Sounds painful."

"Yeah, the last few weeks haven't been the most pleasant."

"I'm sorry to hear that." She took a few steps toward the driveway. "Listen, I was just heading out, so I can't really chat."

He reached forward and touched her elbow. "It was… great to see you again. Maybe we can grab coffee soon or something. Catch up. You know—for old times' sake."

"Maybe." She returned her sunglasses to her face and shot him a brief smile, then turned and hurried across the freshly trimmed grass to climb into a royal blue SUV.

Natalie Bishop.

Not so much the one who got away.

More like the one who pushed him away, wrecking his heart.

No matter how much he had tried to convince her Ben's accident was just that, she'd continued to blame him for her brother's death.

A loud and slightly off-key rendition of "Happy Birthday" sounded from the backyard.

Forcing his attention away from Nat's taillights disappearing quickly over the hill, Evan turned and reached for River's leash. He edged his way through the crowd, then dropped his right arm around his dad's shoulders and chimed in on the last few words.

Dressed in an untucked light blue short-sleeved button-down shirt, khaki shorts, and his ever-present white socks and white sneakers combo, Dad turned. Tall and thin with short, graying hair and weathered skin that showed his love of the outdoors, a huge grin split his face. "Evan!"

He wrapped Evan in a hug so tight he sucked air through clenched teeth once again.

For a moment, though, he allowed himself to relax and forget about the last four weeks, and how anxiety and loneliness had taken up residence in his soul.

Dad released him and looked at him through misty eyes. Then, noticing the sling bracing his left arm against his body, he frowned. "What happened?"

Before he could respond, his older brothers, Jake and Tucker, rallied around them with Jake's pregnant wife, Tori, and Tucker's fiancée, Isabella, shadowing them. His six-year-old twin niece and nephew, Olivia and Landon, barreled into his legs. "Uncle Evan!"

He knelt on the grass and wrapped both of them in a one-armed hug. "Hey, monkeys. I think you've grown two feet since I saw you last."

Livie, her blond hair pulled into a ponytail, grinned, exposing missing teeth. She cupped his cheek. "Uncle Evan, you're so silly. We were born with two feet."

"What happened to your arm?" Landon pointed to the blue sling.

"While practicing for a race, I cared more about my buddy gaining on me than watching where I was going. I hit a dead tree in the water and flipped my kayak, dislocating my shoulder. I had surgery about a month ago."

"Surgery? Why didn't you say something? I would have been there for you." Dad frowned. Despite his level tone, Evan heard what he wasn't saying.

Yeah, he should have called and told him about the surgery. But it was his mess. He couldn't depend on anyone else to help fix his problems.

Evan pushed to his feet. "You have enough to worry about with the Fatigues to Farming program starting up."

Dad gave him a pointed look. "You're my son. Nothing is more important than family. Nothing."

Glancing at the people watching them, Evan shrugged and tried not to wince. He wanted to believe his father's words, but experience had taught him he was better off handling things on his own.

"You always were so independent."

Not always by choice.

Dad pulled him into another hug, gentler this time. Then he grabbed two bottles of water out of the round tub of slushy ice, slid an arm around his shoulders and drew him away from the crowd.

"I'm glad you're home, Ev. How long are you staying?"

Evan let out a breath.

Home.

Where was that exactly?

Even though he'd grown up on the dairy farm, it hadn't quite felt like home since the tornado nearly destroyed the place and killed their mother seven years ago.

Without Mom, his strongest supporter, it just wasn't the same.

Braceleting River's leash, Evan jerked his thumb over his shoulder. "Well, I brought the Water Wagon, so I guess I'm like a turtle—my home is always with me."

Dad handed him one of the bottles of water. "That's great when you're on the road, chasing after competitions, but for as long as you're here, stay at the farmhouse and let us take care of you. You know Claudia won't have it any other way."

As if on cue, his stepmother's infectious laughter caught the breeze. Marrying Evan's mother's best friend since college had been good for his dad...for both of them. He and Claudia understood grief and the beauty of second chances.

Evan's gaze drifted toward the old farmhouse that had been in the family for three generations, untouched by the tornado's destruction.

He didn't want to refuse the invitation, but he'd kind of gotten used to coming and going whenever he wanted since leaving home to fulfill his paddling dreams. And, well, the RV had become his refuge when he couldn't sleep and the walls started closing in. During those nights, he'd climb on top and stretch out under the stars to level out his breathing.

He couldn't do that from inside the farmhouse.

"Thanks, Dad. I don't want to put you out. I'll park the Water Wagon on my piece of property and stay out of everyone's way." Evan uncapped the water bottle and downed half of the icy liquid.

Dad pointed the bottle at him. "You're never in the way. I want you here. For as long as you want to stay."

What Evan wanted and what he'd settled for had been two different things.

Evan swallowed an uncharacteristic lump in his throat and lifted his eyes to the apple orchard hemming the backyard, branches heavy with ripening fruit. "Thanks, Dad."

As if sensing Evan's shift in emotions, River leaned against his leg and Evan ran his fingers over the dog's fur.

"You're good with him." Dad lowered to his haunches and rested his elbows on his knees.

Evan patted River's side. "He's a good boy. Found him abandoned by the river about six months ago, half-starved. Not sure which one of us rescued the other."

"He knows your triggers."

"Triggers for what?"

His father eyed him. "Don't play me, Ev. I may be getting older, but I'm no fool. River senses your anxiety and calms you."

Heat flashed across Evan's face. And here he thought he was coming off cool and collected. He never could pull a fast one on his dad.

"After the accident…"

Evan's heart rate picked up as the memory of the roaring water thundered in his ears, crashing over him. His kayak flipping. He plunged beneath the surface, slamming his head and shoulder against an underwater rock. His foot caught in the downed tree limbs. Pinned. Trapped.

Surges of water choked his throat. Couldn't breathe. Air. He needed air.

"Evan. You okay?"

Something wet and warm nudged his hand.

Evan's eyes flew open.

Early-evening sunshine and farmland replaced the churning icy river.

Dad watched him, deep lines etching his forehead and bracketing his mouth.

Pulling in ragged breaths, Evan scrubbed a shaking hand over his face, his skin slick and clammy. He forced his heaving chest to calm and reached for River once again.

Evan's gaze darted around the farm, taking in guests playing cornhole, children racing with the family dogs, people sitting in lawn chairs under the shade trees. He settled on his father's worried face.

With his arms crossed over his chest, Dad frowned.

"How long have you been experiencing PTSD symptoms?"

"PT—what? No way. Not me." Evan shook his head, then dropped his gaze to the grass. "I've never served in the military. They wouldn't take me, remember?"

Another reminder he didn't fit in with his God-loving, country-serving family.

"Servicemen and -women aren't the only ones who deal with PTSD. Any kind of trauma can cause it. Including an accident. And the way River just responded to you makes me think you could be an asset to a side project we're developing within our Fatigues to Farming program if you're planning to stay awhile."

"How so?"

"Tuck's sister-in-law, Willow, approached us about partnering with Zoe Sullivan at Canine Companions and training her rescued dogs to be paired with veterans going through our program."

"Dad, I'm a paddler, not a dog trainer."

Was a paddler.

"You're an animal whisperer—you always have been. Even growing up, when you became too stressed out, we could find you outside romping with the dogs, petting calves inside the barn and brushing down the horses. Planning to stick around for a bit?"

Evan nodded toward his sling. "Can't paddle with a bum shoulder. I need this for a couple more weeks, then I'll go through physical therapy to regain range of motion in my arm. With this season definitely cut short for me, I figured I'd hang out with the family for a while and see what my future holds."

Dad placed a large, callused hand on the back of Evan's neck and gave it a gentle squeeze. "I'm sorry.

I know what being on the water means to you. I wish you'd told me about your accident. No one should go through that alone. I would've been there for you."

"Thanks, Dad. But you have a lot going on right now."

"Like I said—there's nothing more important than family. Remember that. What do you think about working with Zoe and Natalie, and helping us to develop this component of the program?"

If he wasn't on the water, his next favorite place was hanging out with River, who didn't judge him for all the failures in his life.

He glanced at Dad. "Natalie who?"

"Bishop. You two were close once, weren't you?"

At the confirmation of her name, his heart jammed in his throat. For a moment, he allowed himself to remember the softness of her skin, the way her ponytail brushed her graceful neck and the flicker that sparked in her eyes when she'd asked about his injury. Seconds before she hurried away.

He rubbed a fist over his breastbone. "Close enough that I wanted to marry her. But she blamed me for Ben's death."

"You didn't force Ben to enlist. And what happened in the Middle East wasn't your fault."

"She thinks I talked him into it."

"You and Ben were tight and he listened to you, but the kid made up his own mind."

"After Nat and I broke up, I heard she'd left Shelby Lake. When did she return home?"

"Coach Ted had a heart attack a month or so ago and needed a double bypass. Natalie came home to take over managing the kennels until Ted's recovered. But I hadn't seen her until today when she and Ted visited for a bit. He was getting tired, so they left."

"Yeah, I ran into her as I was coming in. Didn't see Coach, though."

"Perhaps working together will mend fences between the two of you."

"I don't know about that."

Her response to his suggestion of coffee hadn't been too well received.

"Never underestimate the power of God, son. Let's grab some food before Claudia accuses me of keeping you to myself." Dad looped an arm around his shoulders.

Evan grabbed River's leash and his water bottle, and followed his father back to the horde, bracing himself for his stepmother's hug and extraordinary ability to see what he wasn't ready to share.

Maybe coming home wouldn't be so bad.

He could take the next few months to focus on healing. If God wanted to provide a miracle that would return him to the water before the season ended, he wouldn't turn it down.

With his paddling career on hold—maybe permanently—he'd be open to helping his family develop the service dog project for their Fatigues to Farming program. That way, he'd be filling his time with something meaningful rather than feeding his self-pity.

And it would be a great opportunity to show Natalie he wasn't the man she'd known in the past.

Would she even want to know the man he had become?

If he could ever earn her forgiveness, then maybe they could have the future they'd once dreamed about.

* * *

Natalie was about to lose everything.

And she had no one to blame but herself.

She refilled Jasper's stainless steel water bowl and set it inside his freshly cleaned kennel. Then she moved on to April's suite.

After tossing and turning most of the night, Natalie must have finally dozed off in the early-morning hours, just in time to be awakened by her five-thirty alarm.

No matter how busy she stayed with cleaning the individual sleeping suites for the dogs they boarded at Bishop Boarding & Kennels, freshening the dog beds with clean blankets, and refilling their bowls with food and water, she still couldn't get Evan Holland out of her mind.

The man wandered through her dreams like a vagrant.

The town that had once been her sanctuary now felt like a prison. No wonder she had left after ending her relationship with Evan over five years ago. Too many memories.

Since returning after her father's heart attack, she hadn't dared leave their home for fear of running into the Hollands. But soon before closing the veterinary clinic for the weekend, her mother was needed for emergency surgery, so Natalie reluctantly agreed to take her father to Chuck's party, taking solace in the belief that Evan was supposed to be battling the rapids across the country.

Not that she kept track.

Her father followed his career and mentioned it casually every now and then.

Feeling safe from her past for a couple of hours at least, she ventured out so her dad could celebrate his friend's birthday. But the moment she let down her guard, she had run into the one person she hadn't wanted to see.

Literally.

And all the feelings and emotions she kept locked away escaped, nearly crushing her on the drive home. Thankfully, her father, who still tired easily after his surgery, was in the car already and hadn't seen Evan.

She didn't have to hang around for that reunion.

She simply needed to avoid him until he ditched his family for another kayaking adventure. Even though Shelby Lake wasn't that big a town, surely they'd be able to stay out of each other's way. And it wasn't like she had to stay holed up at her parents' house forever. Just until her dad was back on his feet.

Then she could return to the small house she rented from her aunt in southwestern New York, just over the Pennsylvania border, and resume the dog training business she'd been growing over the last few years.

And keep past memories tucked back in the deep corners of her mind where they caused the least amount of pain.

If only it were that easy.

She really needed to stop thinking about Evan.

Yeah, that was like commanding her heart to stop beating.

Having filled the last dog's bowl with fresh water, Natalie left the air-conditioned building and headed for the secured leash-free turf play yard. She guided Jasper, a sable-colored German shepherd, April, a fawn-colored English bulldog, and Gypsy Rose, a tan puggle, back inside to eat breakfast.

Once they had been secured in their suites, she

crossed the yard and headed for the back door that led into the kitchen of her parents' house.

Natalie scrubbed her hands and forearms, then dried them. From the fridge she retrieved a package of turkey bacon, a carton of egg whites, a bag of baby spinach and a container of diced, colored peppers.

She opened the bacon and laid strips on the cast-iron rectangular griddle positioned on the long center burner in the middle of the stove.

The front doorbell rang.

Natalie's heart pulsed against her ribs as her fingers curled around the tongs she used to move the bacon.

Stop. You're safe.

Dropping the tongs on the counter, she flicked off the heat, released a breath and headed to the front door. With hands still trembling slightly, she steeled her spine and opened it.

Willow, her best friend since elementary school and her mother's associate at the veterinary clinic, stood on the black semicircular welcome mat. She was dressed in a cute flowered sundress and pink flats, her white medical jacket hanging over her left arm.

Natalie nearly sagged against the door frame. "Hey, Will. Come in."

Willow stepped inside and lifted her nose, her ponytail brushing against her shoulders. "I smell cookies. You baked."

"Yup, I made oatmeal scotchies last night. I wrapped up a plate of them that Aidan and I will deliver to the clinic after breakfast. But you should be smelling bacon now. I just put some on the griddle."

"Maybe so, but you bake when you're stressed. So what's going on?"

"You have a good nose."

Her friend shot her a grin. "When it comes to cookies, I do."

Natalie led the way into the kitchen and motioned for Willow to sit at the table next to the window looking out into the backyard.

Returning to the stove, Natalie turned on the heat and flipped the bacon. Then she moved to the dog-shaped cookie jar on the opposite counter, put a handful of oatmeal cookies on a plate and placed it on the table in front of her friend.

"You're stalling." Willow fisted a hand on her hip.

Natalie headed to the cabinet by the sink for two mugs and filled them with freshly brewed coffee. She handed one to Willow, who stirred in sugar and creamer. "Evan Holland waltzed in as I was leaving Chuck's party to bring Dad home."

Willow's eyes widened. "How'd that go?"

"As well as you'd expect." After adding milk to her cup, Natalie set her coffee on the counter and turned off the griddle. She quickly chopped spinach leaves, then pulled a skillet out of the cabinet next to the stove and let it heat. She poured in egg whites, and tossed in the spinach and peppers.

Willow broke a cookie in half and nibbled on a corner. "How is he? How did he look? Did you talk to him? Did you have Aidan with you?"

"Aidan spent the afternoon with Aunt Diane. I picked him up after Mom finished her surgery. Evan and I were pleasant, but I didn't stick around for any heart-to-heart conversations." Natalie reached for a spatula and folded the egg whites into an omelet. She slid it onto a plate, trying not to dwell on that initial zing in her stomach at seeing the man who had left her heartbroken a handful of years ago.

Although, noticing his arm in a sling, she did feel bad for his situation and could only imagine what he was feeling being away from the water. The flash of pain in his eyes when he casually mentioned his surgery made Natalie wonder just what had happened. And then when he suggested coffee… Oh, she could not let herself travel down that path again.

"Please tell me you're not still blaming Evan for what happened to Ben?"

She shook her head. "I reacted from a place of pain. Simply put, Evan and I wanted two different things. I wanted roots and security, and Evan wanted adventure."

"Well, now that he's home, maybe you two can let go of the past and see what your futures could hold? Maybe even together?"

Natalie gripped the counter as a still-too-vivid memory of a woman kissing Evan pricked her heart. She shook her head. "There's no future for us. Evan's moved on."

"You don't know that for sure. People do change. But let's not talk about Evan. At least not right now." She finished her cookie, then took a quick drink of coffee. "But I do have some news. That's why I stopped by before going in to work."

"What's that?"

Willow brushed her crumbs onto her napkin, then slid it aside to fold her arms on the table. "Tuck called this morning. He talked with his dad and brother, and they said yes to the service dog project that will coordinate with their Fatigues to Farming program."

"Seriously?"

"Yep. Earlier in the week, I had shared the plan with him, explained partnering with Zoe, then mentioned your name. So once Tuck talked with Jake and Chuck, they were totally on board."

Natalie grinned and threw her arms around her friend. "Wow! I can't believe it. That's the best news I've heard in a while. We've wanted to do a service program like this for so long."

Still holding on to Natalie's arms, Willow took a step back. "But this will mean you staying in Shelby Lake. I know you talked about only being here long enough for your dad to get back on his feet, but if we do this together, I can't have you bailing on me in a month or so when his doctor releases him to return to work. Even though you live only an hour away, it's tough enough with our schedules to coordinate time to work together as it is."

Still grinning from the news, Natalie shook her head. "No, I promise not to bail on you. As much as I love living in that cottage and building my own business up there, I can move here, find a place for Aidan and me, then grow my business while helping my parents. Plus, Aidan loves being so close to them. And if it's a success with the veterans in the Hollands' program, then maybe we can expand our services. I'd love to get therapy dogs into the local schools. I've heard about programs that use them to help children get over their reading anxieties."

Willow glanced at her watch, then drained her coffee. "With my dyslexia, you know I'm all for that. I want to talk more about this and make some plans, but I do need to head in to work early today. Can you meet with Zoe Sullivan and the Hollands on Monday after breakfast?"

"Yes, I'll make sure everything is covered at the kennel and be there as long as I can get someone to care for Aidan."

As if he'd heard his name, her five-year-old with dark tousled curls and bright blue eyes appeared in the kitchen doorway still wearing his Spider-Man pajamas. Rubbing one eye with a fist, he looked at her with a sleepy look. "Mom, can I have cookies for breakfast like Aunt Willow?"

She wrapped her arms around her son and pressed a kiss to his cheek. "Sure, when you become a grown-up like Aunt Willow. For now, you can have something healthier like oatmeal or eggs and bacon like Grandpa."

Aidan eyed the plate on the counter and sighed. "Fine. Can I have cheesy eggs?"

"May I?"

"Yes, you may." He grinned, then giggled.

"Funny kid." She gave him a playful swat on his bottom. "Please wash your hands, then tell Grandpa breakfast is ready."

Willow's phone chimed. She pulled it out of the pocket of her white coat and read the screen, her face twisting into a grimace. "Uh, Nat, Tucker just texted me."

Natalie cracked two eggs in the skillet and scrambled them for Aidan. "Yeah? What's going on?"

"Apparently Chuck talked to Evan during the party, and now he's going to be a part of the project, too."

Natalie's hand tightened on the spatula. She closed her eyes a moment, then turned to face her friend. "You've got to be kidding me."

Willow winced and shook her head. "Sorry. I wish I were."

"What am I going to do now?" Natalie tossed the

spatula on the counter, then yanked open the fridge and snatched the bag of shredded cheese. "How can I work with Evan?"

"It's been more than five years. How long are you going to hold on to the past?"

"But it's my superpower." Natalie made a face and shot her friend a grin, but Willow's raised eyebrow and stern look showed she wasn't amused.

"No, it's your protection against future pain."

"I've had enough for one lifetime, thank you very much." Pressing her back against the sink, Natalie buried her face in her hands. "No, Will, it's not that. Evan is—"

The doorbell rang again, cutting off her words.

Forcing self-control she didn't feel, Natalie brushed past Willow and headed for the living room.

Aidan raced ahead of her. "I got it, Mom."

Before she could stop him, he whipped it open. "Hi."

"Hey, how are you?"

That voice.

Natalie pulled the door even wider and stilled. "Evan."

He was dressed in gray shorts and a white V-necked T-shirt that emphasized his muscular arms, wide chest and tanned skin, and she took in his damp dark hair that tended to curl when it grew longer and bright blue eyes rimmed in navy.

A flutter rose in her chest as her breath caught in her throat.

He stared at Aidan with an indescribable look on his face.

She pushed herself in front of her son, trying to block him from Evan's view. "What are you doing here?"

"I wanted to talk to you and say hi to Coach since I missed seeing him yesterday. Dad told me about his

heart attack and bypass surgery. I'm sorry to hear that."
Even as he spoke, his eyes drifted away from Natalie
and zeroed on Aidan, who was trying to peek around
her legs. He shot her a look she couldn't quite decipher.
"You have a son?"

Clenching her fists, she closed her eyes and pulled
in a lungful of air. Her heart slipped as she opened her
eyes to find Evan watching her intently.

Yep, life as she knew it would never be the same
again.

And she had no one to blame but herself.

Chapter Two

❧

Nat had a kid?

How was that possible?

Did his family know, and no one had said anything to spare his feelings?

No, they wouldn't do that. Especially his father, who valued family and integrity above all else.

Evan rubbed the back of his neck. No wonder she hadn't been too receptive about grabbing coffee.

She'd moved on.

He hadn't seen her since the night of their breakup. A night forever ingrained in his memory.

Seeing her again yesterday had sparked a flicker of hope.

That had been snuffed out the moment her child appeared.

His chest tightened. He rubbed his breastbone with the heel of his hand and tried to look at her fingers without being obvious, but she shoved them into the front pockets of her shorts.

How could he search for a wedding ring?

The little boy, dressed in red-and-blue Spider-Man

pajamas, peered around her legs once again. "What's your name?"

"Hey, buddy, why don't you head upstairs and get dressed?" Nat turned her son's shoulders away from the doorway and then tried to block him from squeezing through again.

Giggling, the little scamp scooted out on his hands and knees between her legs.

She reached down and caught his bare foot.

He turned and glared at her. "Mo-om, no fair."

Evan couldn't help himself and let out a chuckle. "My name's Evan. What's yours?"

He wiggled free of his mother's grasp and stood, giving Evan a shy smile. "Aidan Benjamin Bishop."

Evan dropped to his haunches and held out his hand. "It's nice to meet you, Aidan Benjamin Bishop."

Aidan placed his small hand in Evan's larger one. "You, too. I'm five."

Evan froze, then shot a glance at Nat, whose face drained of color. He forced a casual tone. "Five, huh? That's a supercool age. When's your birthday?"

"February fourteenth. I was Mommy's Valentine's present." He glanced over his shoulder. "Right, Mom?"

"You sure were, buddy. How about heading back inside?"

Evan hadn't been a math genius in school, but he had no problem counting back nine months in his head. He and Natalie were still together at that time.

No.

His mouth went dry. A chill slicked his skin.

No way.

Nat wouldn't keep something like that from him.

Evan scanned her face, but she wouldn't meet his

gaze. He turned back to Aidan and stared at a miniature version of himself with the dark curly hair and blue eyes. Or at least how he'd looked nearly twenty-five years ago.

Pulling in some badly needed air, Evan pushed to his feet and turned away from the kid staring at him with questioning eyes and the woman who had betrayed both of them.

A light wind pushed the front porch swing, releasing a memory of the night they'd sat together, crying after receiving the news about Ben's death.

A hummingbird flitted and sipped nectar from the handblown crimson-colored feeder he'd bought for Natalie after she'd shared how hummingbirds brought her joy. Across the yard, barking came from the kennels behind Dr. Mary's vet office as cars pulled into the paved lot.

So many memories.

Too many.

And not one memory of Natalie letting him know he had a son.

He had to get out of there, but first he needed to know the answer to the question rolling around in his head.

He turned back around and reached for her hand. "Nat, please…please tell me—"

Nat pulled out of Evan's grasp and knelt in front of Aidan, placing her hands on his shoulders. "Aidan, please go into the kitchen and finish your breakfast. Then I want you to go upstairs and get dressed."

"But, Mom—"

"No buts. Please follow directions so you can help Grandpa walk the dogs, okay?"

The kid dropped his chin to his chest, then kicked at the mat edged against the front door with his bare toe. "Fine."

Looking at Evan, he lifted a hand and waved, shooting him a very familiar looking smile. "Bye, Evan. Nice to meet you."

Evan's knees nearly buckled. "You, too, Aidan. See you soon."

Real soon.

Once Aidan disappeared back inside the house, Nat closed the door behind her and faced Evan. She opened her mouth to speak, but then closed it again and sighed, twisting her fingers together.

Her silence told him everything he needed to know.

Without another word, he strode back to the farm truck he'd borrowed that morning to visit the Bishops.

How could she have kept something so important from him?

An ache squeezed his chest.

"Evan," Natalie called as she hurried after him.

Clenching his jaw, he gripped the door handle to stop the trembling in his hands. Forcing himself to take deep, calming breaths, he turned slowly and faced her. "How could you do this to me? Is this payback for Ben's death?"

Sucking in a breath, her eyes widened as she shook her head. "What? No. It's nothing like that."

"Then why didn't you tell me I had a son?" His voice was hoarse and low to his own ears.

Even saying the words made his head spin.

Natalie lowered her gaze and twisted a ring on her finger—not a wedding ring, but the promise ring he'd given her as a placeholder until he could afford to replace it with a real engagement ring. If she wanted nothing to do with him, why did she still wear it?

Lifting her head, she looked at him with what appeared to be pleading eyes.

"Why, Nat?" He scrubbed a hand over his face, his voice rough and thready.

"Evan…" She covered her face a moment, then dropped her hands and looked at him. "I'm sorry. I know that sounds so insignificant now."

Evan scraped a hand over his face and blew out a breath. "That night we—"

She held up a hand, cutting off his words. "Evan, let's not talk about that night."

"You still keep people at a distance, don't you?"

She rubbed one bare foot over the other. "Not purposefully. It's a defense mechanism, I guess."

"Against what?"

"Getting hurt."

He lifted her chin to look into her eyes and gentled his voice. "I'd never hurt you."

"I know you wouldn't intentionally, but you did hurt me when you left." Her words were spoken so low that if he hadn't been looking at her, he would have missed them.

"I'm sorry. I didn't like the way we ended things, either, but we can't change the past." He took a step toward her, then stopped when she backed away. He schooled his tone. "I need to hear you say Aidan is my son."

Biting the corner of her lip, she looked away, not responding. Then she gave him a slight nod as a tear slipped down her cheek.

If someone had slit open his chest, ripped out his heart and slammed it to the ground, it couldn't have hurt any worse.

The wall of pine trees marking the edge of the Bishops' property loomed over him, blocking out the light and squeezing the air from his lungs. "You had no right to keep him from me."

"Were you ready to give up your career and settle down to be a father?"

"I wasn't given the option of making a choice, was I? Besides, a lot of paddlers take their families on the road, homeschooling their children and teaching them the ways of the water. It didn't have to be an either-or situation."

"Yeah, that's what I want for my son—a nomadic lifestyle with no place to call home. I—we—need a permanent address." She folded her arms and jerked her gaze toward the redbrick two-story house with black shutters.

Was that a flicker of fear in her eyes?

"Professional paddlers have permanent homes, Natalie. They travel during the season and make it a family venture. Their kids learn the value of hard work and chasing their dreams." Evan rubbed a finger and thumb over his eyes. "Listen, it's simple—I have a son and you didn't tell me. As his father, I have rights. I do not walk away from my responsibilities."

"You had no problem walking away from me." She turned away, but not before he caught the pain in her face.

He touched her elbow. "*You* pushed *me* away, blaming me for Ben's death, saying we had no future together."

She looked at him again, this time with a steely glare. "If you hadn't talked him into enlisting, he'd be alive today."

"You're not God. You don't know that. We planned to enlist together, but I was disqualified because I was still on medication for my asthma. Ben made his own choice to enlist anyway. He was my best friend. You think I don't miss him every single day?" Evan dragged a hand through his hair. "What you've done is unforgivable, Natalie. I need to go, but this isn't over. Far from it."

Without another look at her, he yanked open the door and jammed himself into the driver's seat. He slammed his palm against the steering wheel. After starting the engine, he peeled out of the driveway, spitting gravel from beneath his tires.

Now that he knew about Aidan, he'd fight Natalie with everything he had. He'd become the best father he could be to the little boy who didn't know he existed.

How was Evan going to tell his family about Aidan?

After leaving the Bishops', he drove around for about an hour to clear his head. Then he tried calling his youngest brother to get some insight. His call went to Micah's too-full voice mail, not allowing him to leave a message. He'd try again later.

Realizing his father or Jake might be waiting for the truck, he headed back to the farm. He pulled into the barnyard and parked, letting the engine idle while he struggled to make sense of what had happened.

The door to the milk house swung open, and his oldest brother, Jake, stepped out. He was dressed in faded jeans, black barn boots and a navy T-shirt with a rip at the hem.

Evan cut the engine and exited the truck, slamming the door a little harder than necessary.

"Hey, man. What's going on?" Jake cocked his head and looked at him. "You okay?"

Evan spun the key ring on his index finger, then

shoved the keys and his hand in his front pockets. "I went to see Natalie Bishop."

Jake let out a low whistle. "Enough said. How'd that go?"

"Definitely not what I expected." Evan jerked his head toward the farmhouse. "You heading inside?"

"To grab a quick cup of coffee. Tori's talking to Dad about some grant she found to help with funding the service dog project. Tuck and Isabella brought the twins down to have breakfast with Dad and Claudia."

Any other time he'd enjoy hanging out with his family, but today he really didn't need an audience to share in his failure. Still, his father needed to know now instead of learning about Aidan from someone else.

Why hadn't Coach said anything? Especially after all these years?

Jake clapped him on the shoulder, and the brothers walked silently through the yard to the back deck. Music and laughter filtered through the screen door. Two things he could always count on when Claudia was around.

They stepped inside to find only Dad and Tucker in the kitchen. Claudia, Tori, Isabella and the twins weren't in sight, but he could hear talking and the sound of the TV coming from the family room.

The kitchen, redone shortly before the tornado hit, had been Mom's dream, though she hadn't lived long enough to enjoy it. Even after Claudia had moved in, she'd changed very little. The white cabinets, subway-tile backsplash and reclaimed barn board countertops invited family to gather together while sharing in cooking and cleanup.

Evan inhaled the scents of freshly brewed coffee,

fried bacon and pancakes with maple syrup tapped from trees on the farm.

Dad looked up from the stove, where he flipped pancakes and then stacked them on a platter. He nodded toward the plates on the counter. "Grab a plate. Coffee's fresh."

Evan fished the keys out of his front pocket and set them on the table that had belonged to Evan's great-grandparents. "Thanks for letting me borrow the truck."

Dad turned off the flame under the square griddle and eyed Evan. "Everything okay, son?"

The same loaded question he'd heard hundreds of times growing up. The calm voice seeking answers without judgment.

Evan looked into his father's eyes, lined with age and experience, then he lowered his gaze to his flip-flops that had seen better days. To his horror, his eyes filled quicker than he could blink away moisture. His chest shuddered as he replayed the shock of seeing Aidan and learning who he was. He cupped a hand over his eyes and choked on a ragged breath as he struggled to regain his composure.

The last thing he needed right now was to fall apart and bawl like a baby in front of his older brothers, who loved to tease him unmercifully.

Dad squeezed his shoulder, which nearly undid him once again.

He ground his thumb and forefinger into his eyes to wick away the moisture. Then he moved to the sink and filled a glass with water. After downing it, he turned to find his father, Jake and Tucker standing identically in front of the kitchen table, feet apart and arms crossed over their chests.

Evan cleared his throat and heaved a sigh as his family watched and waited. "So, I went to the Bishops' to talk to Natalie about the service dog project and to say hi to Coach since I missed seeing him yesterday. But we didn't get a chance to talk."

"Why not?"

"Natalie's son opened the door."

Dad stared at him with a startled expression, then exchanged glances with Jake and Tucker. "Son? I didn't know she had a child. Ted never mentioned it. Not once."

"Maybe for good reason." He blew out a breath. "He probably didn't want you to know."

"Why not? Ted and I have been friends for over forty years."

"The kid's mine, Dad." The words came out in a rush.

A muscle jumped in the side of Dad's jaw, but he didn't say anything. He pressed his back against the fridge, crossed his arms over his chest and looked at Evan with a neutral expression on his face.

Jake and Tucker exchanged wide-eyed glances but remained quiet.

He could only imagine what was going on in their heads.

Dad straightened and slid his fingers into his front pockets. "You and Natalie Bishop had a child together, and she never told you?"

"You think if Natalie had told me about him, I would've kept it from the family?"

Dad shook his head and rubbed a hand over his chin. "How old is this child?"

"Five. His name's Aidan Benjamin Bishop." His lips quirked at the matter-of-fact way Aidan had declared who he was.

"I didn't realize you and Natalie had been…together."

"Once—an unplanned moment after learning about Ben's death. I tried to comfort her…and things got out of hand. We made a mistake." He lowered his head as heat crawled up his neck.

"No. You two made a child. No matter the circumstances, that little boy is a blessing from God. And to our family."

Evan lifted his head and met his father's eyes. "He doesn't even know who I am. If I hadn't come back to town, she would've continued to keep him from me. That's totally unforgivable."

His father rested a hand on his shoulder. "Keeping Aidan from you was wrong on Natalie's part, but it's certainly forgivable."

"Not by me." Evan folded his arms over his chest, suddenly feeling like a pouty preschooler.

"You're upset right now, and rightfully so, but give it some time. We've all done things that don't deserve forgiveness, but God's grace and mercy offers us second chances. You two have a child together, so somehow, you will need to forgive Natalie so you two can co-parent Aidan to the best of your abilities."

Jake cleared his throat and pushed away from the table. "Look, Ev, I know this stinks. And there was a time when I didn't think I could forgive Tori, but we learned how to work it out. And look at us now—we're married with a baby on the way."

His dad and brother were right. After all, biblical values and principles had been drilled into his head since he was younger than Aidan. But, right now, that open wound was still too raw and too fresh to even consider forgiving Natalie.

"So what are you going to do?" Tuck, always the cool and collected one, moved next to Evan and refilled his own coffee mug.

Evan lifted a shoulder and shoved his hand in his front pocket. "Take responsibility for my actions, and be the father my son deserves."

His son.

Man, it seemed so surreal. He didn't deserve a kid like Aidan. The boy needed more than a screwup for a father.

But he wanted to get to know him.

So, he'd man up and do whatever it took to prove he could be the kind of father Aidan needed. Even if it meant calling some sort of truce with Natalie.

Forgiving her, on the other hand, was another matter altogether.

Chapter Three

Natalie needed to make amends.

Somehow, she had to convince Evan she hadn't kept Aidan from him out of spite. Or that it had anything to do with her brother's death.

The look on his face that morning when he learned about Aidan would be imprinted forever in her memory.

No matter what she said, though, he wouldn't believe her right now. He was too angry.

She valued the importance of having a good father in her life. So why had she denied Aidan the same thing?

A light tapping sounded on the front door.

Alice, her parents' brown-and-white collie, lifted her head off Natalie's knee, then bounded off the couch for the door.

Natalie closed her laptop, set it on the coffee table in front of the couch and headed for the door. A glance through the peephole showed Evan standing on the porch.

She sighed.

Sure, she wanted to make amends. But after she'd

had time to come up with a plan and they had set up a meeting on neutral territory.

So much for that idea.

Flipping on the porch light, she opened the door, a humid breeze whisking over her face. A storm was coming.

"Evan. What are you doing here?"

He palmed the door frame and gave her a tired look. "Can we talk?"

Running a hand over her hair, she nodded and moved back to allow him to enter the house, wishing someone else had answered the door. That would have given her the opportunity to escape or at least change into something more presentable than an old T-shirt left over from high school and jean shorts with frayed hems. "Come in."

"I'd rather stay out here. This won't take long." He stepped back to rest a shoulder against one of the columns lining the covered porch. The light blue T-shirt tightened across his muscled chest.

Quickly trying to gather some thoughts, she stepped outside, closing the door behind her, and gestured toward the matching padded chairs where her parents relaxed in the evenings after work. She settled in her mom's spot, picked up a throw pillow of a yellow sunflower and hugged it to her chest.

Evan remained standing.

Darkening clouds smudged the sky, pushing out the daylight to shroud them in the shadows. The porch light glow cast over Evan emphasized his set jaw and stiff posture.

Pushing away from the column, he ran a hand across the back of his neck. "I don't want to fight with you, Nat.

That's not who I am. And it's not healthy for any of us. But we need to reach some sort of agreement so I can get to know my son."

His matter-of-fact tone cinched the knot in her stomach.

He was right.

And she wanted what was best for Aidan—for all of them.

But…

She breathed in slowly and released the air to calm the rising anxiety in her chest. She twisted her fingers together to stop their trembling.

Natalie looked at Evan and forced a smile. "What do you have in mind?"

Evan crossed the porch, sat on the edge of the chair next to her and rested his elbows on his knees. "Time. I want to spend time with Aidan and get to know him. And I want to help provide for him financially."

"What about your career?"

He frowned. "What about it?"

She toyed with the manufacturer's tag on the throw pillow. "How can you be a paddler and a father?"

"Like I told you yesterday—it's not an either-or situation, Nat. I can do both."

"You're making a name for yourself. Your face was on a national magazine a couple of months ago." Natalie dropped the pillow onto the porch floor and pushed to her feet. Folding her arms over her chest, she turned to face Evan. "He doesn't need that kind of exposure."

Evan held up a finger. "First of all, it was one cover. I'm a nobody who got lucky one time and managed to get my face on the cover of a magazine only paddlers or water enthusiasts read." He lifted another finger. "And second, I can keep my private life separate from my professional life."

"Keeping Aidan safe is my number one priority."

"Of course. Isn't that every parent's goal? But I can keep him safe just as well as you can, Nat." Standing, Evan slid a hand over his face.

"How long are you planning to be in Shelby Lake?"

He lifted a shoulder and flinched. "I'm not sure yet. My paddling days are pretty much over for the rest of the season. Maybe for good—I don't know. I'll have to see how my PT goes. For now, though, I'm back home. You have twenty-four hours to consider my request and make a choice. Nat, please don't make this any more difficult than it needs to be. Despite what you may think of me, I will be a great father. Just give me a chance to prove it. You owe me—and Aidan—that."

Without another word, he headed down the steps, pulling the truck keys out of his pocket. Once he'd backed out of the driveway and disappeared down the road, Natalie dropped back into her mother's chair and buried her face in her hands.

"Hey, you okay?"

Natalie looked up to find her mother, dressed in paw-print pajamas, standing in the doorway. With her dark wavy hair pulled back into a low ponytail and her freshly washed face free of lines and makeup, she looked more like an older sister than her mother.

She shook her head and swallowed past the pressure in her throat.

"What's going on?" Mom stepped onto the porch and sat on the swing, giving it a little push with her bare foot.

Natalie recapped her discussion with Evan. "I just want to take Aidan and run."

"Running isn't the answer. You know that," her mother said. "What are you afraid of?"

"You know what, Mom." She lowered her voice to a whisper. *"Him."*

"Oh, honey, Evan is nothing like Brady."

Natalie's eyes widened as she looked over her shoulder. "Don't ever say that man's name. What kind of father deserts his children? Or his wife? Leaving her with nothing but a destructive trail of empty promises and debts. We lost everything, including our house, because of him. And you nearly lost Ben and me because we were sleeping in the car."

"Sweetheart, that was twenty years ago. We're safe now. It's past time to stop looking over your shoulder and realize you're safe from him. Brady can't hurt you or me anymore."

Natalie blinked rapidly to hold back the tears threatening to flood her eyes. Her hair fell forward, curtaining her view of her mother. "I'll stop when he's buried. He vowed to find us, remember? He blames you for his arrest and promised to make us pay. How can you *not* look over your shoulder, waiting and wondering? Until then, I'll do whatever it takes to protect my son."

"Those were the rantings of an angry, narcissistic man. We moved across the country and changed our names. He will not find us. Protecting yourself and Aidan has nothing to do with Evan."

"Evan landed on the cover of one magazine already. What if he does well in his career and makes it big? What if there's more media coverage? What if people discover he has a son? What if *he* reads an article and finds out where we are?" Natalie's voice rose as her chest heaved.

She was being irrational, but how did she stop listening to the "what if" questions that had plagued her over and over? The questions had fed her fears and deepened her anxieties until she was afraid of saying the wrong thing and losing everything all over again.

The swing creaked as her mother got off it and knelt in front of Natalie, wrapping her in her arms. "Honey, that has nothing to do with anything. You can't keep Aidan from his own father. Your father and I have been against that from the moment you told us you were pregnant. Evan's a good man who won't hurt either of you. Tell him what happened. I'm sure he'll be more than understanding. And it will help you two to bridge this gap so you can be the best parents possible for Aidan. Isn't he what matters the most in this situation? It's time to stop running."

How could she do something she'd perfected over the past two decades?

But her mother was right—Aidan was her priority. She had to figure out how to move past her fears in order to create a future her son deserved.

Somehow, she had to make it work.

No matter what it cost her.

House hunting took a new level of patience Evan wasn't quite sure he possessed.

But if he wanted to prove to Natalie that he could be a responsible father to Aidan, he needed to find a different place to live. His son needed more than a tricked-out RV to call home.

Problem was, Evan wanted to live on Holland Hill— on the property his dad had given him after dividing the farmland into five sections. A portion was to be used

in some way for the Fatigues to Farming program—
a condition each person received upon accepting their
early inheritance. Evan's lot bordered Arrowhead Creek,
which flowed through their land. When Evan revealed
he didn't know what he could do for the program, his
father had said God would offer the answer when the
time was right.

While he'd traveled on the kayaking pro tour, his
lot had sat vacant. Now that he was home—maybe for
good—he needed to figure out permanent digs. He had
more than enough space for a house and a yard for his
family.

Family.

Man, that still blew his mind.

After church, he'd spent some time doing online research. He closed his laptop and skimmed the pages of
notes. He had two choices—building from the ground
up or buying a prefabricated house that would be built
in a factory, transported on semis and put together in
place. The second option might be faster and less ex-
pensive than constructing a home on-site.

He'd have to look into financing and find a good company to work with. These were things that took more
time than he wanted, but he couldn't snap his fingers
and have a house put up overnight.

Even though car dealerships were closed, he could
cruise by a couple of lots and see what was available.
He needed his own wheels even sooner than the house.

Although borrowing the truck was fine now and then,
it was needed for farmwork. The last thing Evan wanted
was to rely on someone else anyway.

Since he hadn't seen Ted at the early church service

Evan had attended with his family, he wanted to swing by and say hi to his former mentor.

Which meant seeing Natalie again.

Less than ten minutes later, Evan pulled into the Bishops' driveway and cut the engine. As he climbed out from behind the wheel, Ted Bishop, Evan's former swim coach and mentor, rounded the side of the kennel. He walked a leashed black dog with a white eye patch.

Seeing Evan, he lifted a hand and waved.

Evan jogged across the grass and greeted him with a one-armed hug. "Hey, Coach."

"Evan, my man. So good to see you." Coach clapped him on the back.

"How's it going?" Evan frowned at the frailness of the once-healthy man who used to swim miles each day.

The dog by Coach's side sniffed Evan's shoes and jeans, probably detecting River's scent, then wagged his tail and looked up at Evan with large brown eyes. Evan cast a glance at Coach. "May I?"

"Sure, go ahead. Petey's a very friendly dog. He's one of our boarders this week while his family's on vacation."

Evan patted Petey's neck. "Hey, you're a good boy, aren't you?"

"You're good with animals. Always have been."

"Animals don't betray you. They're loyal and just want to be loved."

"Our friend Zoe Sullivan says the same thing." Coach led Petey to a fenced-in turf play yard and unclipped the dog's leash. Once Petey had bounded over to play with the other dogs, Coach secured the gate and turned back to Evan, leveling him with a stare he'd seen too many

times in his life. "How've you been? Judging by that
sling, I take it paddling is on hold for now?"

Evan glanced down at his arm. "Another dislocated
shoulder, which required surgery this time."

"Sorry to hear that. I've read your magazine articles and caught your recent cover story. Nice job. Your
old man and I watched a couple of your races together.
You're good."

"Apparently not good enough to know I should have
zigged instead of zagged." Or paid more attention to his
own paddling instead of worrying about the other guy.

Coach clamped a hand on Evan's good shoulder and
gave it a light squeeze. "Hey, it happens to the best of
them. Don't beat yourself up. As much as I'm happy
to see you, I'm guessing you didn't stop by to see me."

"Actually, I did. I attended the early service with Dad
and Claudia and didn't see you there. Although I've been
by a couple of times and I've wanted to say hi, once
Nat and I started talking about Aidan…" Sighing, he
shrugged.

"Mary and I went to the later service. It's the one day
of the week she can sleep in a little, so I try to protect
that time if I can."

"You're a good man, Coach." Evan shoved his hand
in his pocket and scanned the driveway, not seeing Natalie's car.

As if reading his mind, Coach said, "She's not here.
She took Aidan up to their cottage to start packing."

Busted.

"Do you know when she's going to be back? After
catching up with you, I was hoping to chat with her.
Since we're going to be working together, I don't want
anything weird between us."

"It's probably going to be weird between you two until you can get things worked out." Coach rubbed a hand over his chin. "I'm sorry you didn't know about Aidan until now. I may not have agreed with my daughter's choices, but I had to respect her wishes."

"What reason is good enough to keep a child from his father? I'm a pretty decent guy—you can vouch for my character, Coach. I just don't get it."

He shot Evan a direct look. "You need to talk to Natalie. There's more going on here than I can share."

"I think I'd get more answers from Petey than from your daughter." Evan glanced back at the farm truck. "I should go. Maybe working together isn't the best idea."

"I'd like you to reconsider. Natalie needs you as much as you need her."

Evan shook his head. "I don't need anyone."

"Baloney. We all need people in our lives. God created us for relationships—with him and with others. I admire you, Evan." He held his hand out about waist high. "I still remember the first time I met you—a skinny little five-year-old standing at the edge of the pool afraid to jump in. But you did it. And look at you now. You faced your fears. And I really appreciate what you've done for us."

Evan cracked a smile as the faded memory of that day filtered through his head. Then he looked at Coach and lifted a shoulder. "I haven't done anything."

"Oh, really, Iris?"

Evan stuffed his hand in his pocket, trying to appear casual. He raised an eyebrow. "Iris?"

Coach laughed and shook his head. "Don't play me, son."

Dropping his gaze to the ground, Evan scuffed the toe of his flip-flop against the grass. "How did you know?"

"You and Ben were as thick as thieves. I loved you as if you were my own son. I knew your potential, and I've been following your career. We'd had no known association with an Iris Buchanan in the past so when this mysterious benefactor started sending money for the Benjamin Bishop Scholarship Fund each time you won a tournament, I put two and two together."

Evan rubbed a hand over the back of his head. "Okay, you got me. Mind keeping this between us?"

"Secrets can be more harmful than helpful."

"Ben and I—we loved the water. Some of my favorite memories include paddling around the lake or down the river with him. When I didn't qualify for the Marine Corps, he encouraged me to pursue a paddling career, even though I was so sure I was going to fail miserably and come home a loser. But Ben—he had more confidence in me than I had in myself. I figured I could honor his memory by offering hope to someone else trying to pursue their dreams."

Coach clapped him on the back. "Like I said—you're a good man, Evan."

Evan lifted a corner of his mouth. "You may want to share that info with your daughter."

"Oh, she knows. She just needs to work through some stuff to let others close."

Natalie's SUV pulled in behind the farm truck. She stepped out from the driver's side wearing jeans, a red scoop-neck T-shirt and her oversize sunglasses. Seeing Evan, she stiffened, then opened the back door.

A moment later, Aidan scrambled out and raced over

to Coach, flinging his arms around the man's legs. "Hi, Grandpa."

Shooting a glance at Evan, Coach lifted the child in his arms. "Hey, A-man. What's happening?"

Instead of answering, Aidan scrambled out of Ted's arms and stood in front of Evan. His small hands fisted on his hips, and he scowled at him. "You made my mom cry. I don't like you."

He appreciated the kid's desire to protect his mom, but the words still stung.

Evan glanced at Natalie, who had pushed her sunglasses on top of her head and looked away. He crouched in front of his son. "I'm sorry I made your mom cry. I don't like hurting people. I promise not to hurt her again…at least on purpose. Will you forgive me?"

Aidan eyed him. "You promise?"

"Cross my heart." Evan x-ed his chest, then stuck out his hand.

Aidan put his small hand in Evan's large one, and something inside Evan's chest broke free at the innocent trust in his son's eyes.

Evan wanted to haul the boy into a hug, but he didn't want to freak him out. After all, Aidan didn't even know who Evan was. Somehow, he and Nat had to make this work because Evan wasn't going anywhere.

Evan pushed to his feet. "Nat, can I talk to you a minute?"

Nat glanced at Aidan and Ted, back at him and nodded. "Sure."

Coach put his hand on Aidan's shoulder. "Let's go make sure the dogs have plenty of water."

"Okay, Grandpa." Aidan ran ahead to the kennels with Coach trailing in his dust.

Once they were out of earshot, Evan turned to Natalie. "What did you decide?"

She set her sunglasses back on her nose. "We need to work out an agreement between us that won't involve the courts, but before we do that, I have a few conditions of my own."

"Like what?"

"Temporary supervised visitation to ensure you can handle Aidan."

"What? No way."

Did she think he was that incompetent?

Natalie held up a hand. "Let me finish."

"Fine."

"Like I said—temporary. Just until you two can get to know each other."

Evan ground his jaw, fighting back words he really wanted to say—words that would only widen the rift between them.

"And your other conditions?"

"You and your family aren't allowed to bad-mouth me in front of Aidan."

Evan raised an eyebrow. "Have you met my family? My dad doesn't say anything bad about anyone."

"I know, I just wanted to make it clear."

"Well, you have nothing to fear from me or my family. We don't play that way."

"Thank you."

"So when do these supervised visitations begin?"

"You're always welcome here. Aidan can stay with you when you have a suitable place for him to sleep. Are you staying at the farm?"

"Sort of. I crash in the RV, but I shower at the farmhouse and eat most meals with Dad and Claudia. I'm working on a permanent housing situation."

"I'm not asking for anything from you, but I would like to know if you're able to help support him."

"Of course." Evan lifted his left arm, still in the sling, and winced a little. "Until this is healed, I'm off the water, but I have money saved. And I write articles for paddling and water sports magazines. It's not going to make me rich, but I won't starve, either. Don't worry, I can take care of my son."

"*Our* son. And have you met me? *Worry* is my middle name. I just want to make sure Aidan's taken care of when he's with you."

"I promise you—he will be fine. Are you living with your parents?"

She waved a hand toward her parents' property. "Temporarily. I came home after Dad's heart attack to help manage the kennels. Even though he's been improving daily, he still tires quickly these days. I'm a little concerned."

"He's not coaching anymore?"

"Well, with school out for the summer, he's had a reprieve. His doctor will re-evaluate him before school resumes and let him know if he can return to work."

"I'm sorry, Nat. That's tough."

She nodded. "Yes, it is, but he's alive. That's the important thing."

"You said 'temporarily.' Once your dad returns to work, are you leaving?"

Nat lifted a shoulder and sighed. "No. My address is still in New York—I've been renting a cottage from my aunt, but now that your family is invested in this service dog project, I'll be looking for a place here for Aidan and me to live. I've been helping Mom and Dad, but we can't stay here forever. Aidan will begin kindergarten at Shelby Lake Elementary in a few weeks."

"So it looks like we're both trying to figure out our permanent places in life. You listed your conditions, so I'd like to add one of my own. Beginning today, anything involving Aidan needs to be discussed before a decision is made. I want equal say in his health care, education, everything. That way, we're both on the same page."

"That sounds fair." She placed a hand on his forearm, her soft touch warm against his skin. "Evan, again, I'm sorry. I did it to protect my son."

Aidan's laughter traveled across the grass from where he sat in the play yard getting licked by Petey. Evan pulled his attention back to Natalie. "*Our* son. I appreciate the apology, Nat, but I gotta be honest—I'm still struggling with the reason why. You say you did it for Aidan—I can't help wondering if you did it more to protect yourself."

Chapter Four

Sleeping on it was supposed to give Natalie a fresh perspective.

At least that was the advice her father had offered her so many times through the years when she'd wrestled with a problem.

But from the moment Evan returned home, her perspective had been chased away by memories that refused to be leashed—memories she tried so hard to keep locked away because they were too painful.

Why did Evan have to come home anyway?

Everything was going well until he showed up.

Wasn't it?

Even though she tried to keep her fears and anxieties from interfering with her daily living, putting on a happy face for others was exhausting.

And now with Evan back in the picture, her carefully constructed life had been shredded like the cheap dog toy that Daisy, one of the cocker spaniels at Canine Companions—Zoe Sullivan's rescue shelter—had dropped at Natalie's feet before settling into her lap.

Evan kept asking questions she wasn't ready to answer.

Sitting on the sun-warmed grass inside the gated play yard at the newly expanded Canine Companions Rescue Shelter, Natalie longed to lean back on her arms, lift her face to the midmorning sun, breathe in the clean air and know everything would work out.

But she wasn't wired that way.

And life proved way too often that things didn't always work out.

Instead of spiraling down into a funk, Natalie rested her arm over Daisy, who was nestled her in lap. They sat beneath the shade tree along with Zoe, her father and Evan. She tried to focus on what Zoe was sharing about the fostering component of the service dog project.

With Evan sitting close enough for her to smell his soap and feel the occasional brush of his arm against hers, she struggled to pay attention.

"Natalie." Dad, sitting in a lawn chair on the other side of her, snapped his fingers in front of her face. "Zoe's asked you the same question twice."

Heat warmed her cheeks. "Sorry, Zoe. I was thinking about something else."

"You did look like you were in your own world." Her friend smiled, flicking her chestnut-brown ponytail over her shoulder. "Would you prefer working with a puppy or one of the surrendered dogs we determined to be a good fit for the project?"

"I'll take Daisy. Her sweet eyes get to me every time." Natalie cupped her hand under the dog's chin and rubbed a gentle hand over her butterscotch-colored muzzle.

"Great choice. What about you, Evan?"

"I'll take Toby. He's getting along well with River already." He patted the two-year-old black Lab lying next to River and resting his head on Evan's leg.

"Excellent. They're both great dogs. Daisy's owner moved into a retirement community that doesn't allow pets. Toby was brought into the shelter a few months ago after being found behind a dumpster. He was full of fleas and had a few cuts and scrapes. He's looking to be loved."

Zoe handed each of them a folder. "This is more information about our fostering program. Read through it, write down any questions you may have, and we'll meet again on Friday to begin our first class. Then you can take the dogs home with you, and care for and socialize them over the next three months. After that, we'll re-evaluate. If you'd like to continue with the project, we'll move you into the next phase. In the meantime, get your homes set up for another dog. Any questions?"

Even though she was perfectly content to sit in the shade for the rest of the afternoon with Daisy napping in her lap, Natalie rousted the drowsy dog so she could stand. She brushed grass off the back of her shorts. "What happens once they finish the fostering phase?"

"We will match them with one of the veterans in the Fatigues to Farming program who qualify for a service dog and transition the training to happen between the dog and its permanent owner." Zoe picked up a worn tennis ball one of the dogs had dropped at her feet and tossed it toward the back of the yard.

Toby's head shot up. He jumped to his feet and bounded after the ball.

Evan stood, reached for River's leash, then waved a hand over the dogs. "What happens if either dog doesn't work out for the next phase of the project?"

"Because you're the foster parents, you or Natalie will be given first choice at adoption. If that doesn't work out, then the dog will return to us to be adopted by another family."

The idea of giving Daisy up twisted Natalie's heart. Even though she'd just met her, she felt a connection. She knew the pain of losing everything and starting over. Life needed to be more than temporary. They needed forever homes.

After concluding their meeting, Natalie reluctantly returned Daisy to Zoe's care and pulled her keys out of her front pocket.

Evan touched her elbow, his warm fingers barely a caress against her skin, and leaned in close. "Hey, mind meeting me at Joe's Diner? There's something I'd like to show you."

Her fingers tightened around her keys. He probably wanted to ask more questions she wasn't ready to answer.

Needing a break from Evan's presence, she tried to muster her most apologetic look. "Sorry, I can't. I need to drop Dad off, pick up Aidan from Willow's, then get back to help walk the dogs we're boarding this week."

Although Evan kept a smile in place, a muscle in the side of his jaw tightened. He shoved his hand in the front pocket of his olive green shorts and gave her a nod. "Some other time, then."

After talking to Zoe, her father folded his chair and walked over to them with it under his arm. "Some other time for what?"

Before she could say anything, Evan repeated their conversation.

Dad removed his baseball hat and scratched the top of his hat. "Nonsense. Natalie, drop me off at the house and call Willow to see if she can keep Aidan a little longer."

Was that a smug look on Evan's face as he opened the passenger door of his truck for River to jump up into?

Natalie and her father headed back to her SUV, and as soon as he had snapped his seat belt into place, Natalie turned to him. "Dad, why are you doing this?"

He frowned. "Doing what?"

"Pushing Evan and me together."

He feigned an innocent look that didn't contain the slight smile edging at the corners of his mouth. "I'm doing nothing of the sort."

She shook her head and rolled her eyes. "Whatever."

"Natalie Grace, Evan's a very good man, and you know it. You're just too blind to your own pain to see it. You need someone strong like him in your life."

"I have you."

He rubbed his forehead, looking weary. "I'm not the man I used to be. The heart attack took a lot out of me."

Her hands tightened on the steering wheel, remembering her mother's frantic phone call from inside the ambulance as they transported her barely conscious father to the emergency room. She'd never forget the hours and the waiting and the pacing until they learned he'd barely survived the emergency double bypass surgery.

Natalie reached over and touched her father's shoulder. "You're still a strong man on the inside, and you'll get your strength back."

He had to.

She couldn't imagine life without him.

After dropping off her dad back at the house and calling Willow to keep Aidan a little longer, Nat pulled into the parking lot in front of Joe's Diner. The climbing heat blasted her as she stepped out of her air-conditioned car.

She headed into Joe's, greeted by the scents of grilled

burgers and fresh coffee. Pausing at the door and giving her eyes a moment to adjust to the change in lighting, she scanned the recently remodeled dining room for Evan.

Spying him, she strode past the counter, where sounds from the kitchen filtered through and mingled with chatter from the diners. She slid into the booth across from Evan. He was bent over papers spread out on the table and River was curled up at his feet, away from the flow of traffic.

"Hey."

He looked up and gave her a smile that sent her heart crashing into her rib cage. "Hey, yourself. I'm glad you came."

"Not sure I had much choice."

He frowned. "Of course you did. Life is all about making choices."

"That sounds like something from a fortune cookie." Knowing she needed to show she was trying, she folded her arms on the table and looked at him. "Would you like to come over this evening and hang out? Get to know Aidan a little more? We could make root beer floats."

"Sure, that sounds great." He shot her another grin, then turned a colorful brochure around so she could see what he was reading. "What do you think about this?"

Before she could respond, a server approached to take their drink order. Evan looked at her and raised an eyebrow. "Nat?"

"Just iced tea for me, please."

"Same for me. And a plate of Joe's garbage fries to share."

The thought of Joe's garbage fries smothered in his homemade chili and piled with melted cheddar made her mouth water, although consuming them offered little grace to her waistline.

The server smiled and slid her notepad in the front pocket of her apron. "Great. I'll have those out to you right away."

Natalie turned her attention to the front of the brochure that advertised a company specializing in prefabricated houses. They showcased a gorgeous two-story home with an attached garage, a wide covered front porch and a beautifully landscaped yard with a poured sidewalk curving to the concrete driveway. The sage-green siding with chestnut-brown shutters and twin dormers gave the house a refined elegance. She looked up to find Evan watching her. "It's beautiful."

Evan leaned across the table and opened the brochure. "Check out this floor plan. Vaulted foyer with high ceilings, an open kitchen with an island and a separate dining nook, a living room with a stone fireplace, another living space with French doors that could be a playroom, home office or a family room. On the second floor, there's a master suite, plus two more bedrooms, a second bathroom and a laundry room."

"Like I said, it's gorgeous. But why are you showing this to me?"

Evan settled back into the corner of the booth, leaning a shoulder against the wall. "Because if you approve, then I'm going to buy it and have it built on my property to live in."

"Why do you need my approval?"

"Because we agreed all decisions about Aidan would be made together. I'm hoping this will ease your anxieties a little." Evan's quiet words caught her attention.

She glanced up from the brochure and her gaze tangled with his. Was that vulnerability in his blue eyes?

"I'm touched by your willingness to get my approval in spite of...well, you know. The house is perfect, Evan. In fact..." Her voice trailed off as she returned her attention to the pictures inviting her to spend more time in the rooms.

"What?"

"It's the kind of house I've always dreamed of living in someday."

What if she hadn't pushed Evan away all those years ago? What if she had trusted him to be the keeper of her secrets and protector of her heart? What if she had allowed herself to lean on someone other than her parents?

If she had, would they have had this house already, filling it with children they had planned on having?

Well, that wasn't the case for them.

Because she *had* pushed Evan away. And kept his son from him.

And after what she'd done, he couldn't forgive her.

Without forgiveness, they couldn't have a fresh start.

No, this beautiful home would be a great place for Evan and Aidan, with no place for her.

Once again, she'd be on the outside looking in because her fears held her back.

Evan didn't belong here.

He'd spent countless times in the Bishops' cozy living room with two identical red reclining couches separated by a heavy rectangular coffee table, walls painted the color of vintage paper and a stone fireplace flanked by built-in bookcases.

He'd never felt as uncomfortable as he did this evening.

He'd rather be outside or at the kennel assisting with the dogs. This was the first time he'd spent any length of time in the living room since Ben's death.

Dressed in a white cover and navy Marine Corp blues blouse, Ben's solemn face in his boot camp picture stared at him from the mantel. The framed photo sat next to the folded American flag in the polished oak case given to his parents at his funeral with full military honors.

Another life-changing moment in Evan's life.

But, despite the tornado that had ravaged his family's farm and killed his mother, losing his best friend, breaking up with the woman he loved and now his shoulder injury, nothing compared to learning he was a father.

To a kid who didn't know him.

At the diner earlier in the afternoon, Nat had invited him over after dinner to visit for a while to get to know Aidan.

But Aidan didn't seem to be in a hurry to get to know him.

When Evan arrived, Aidan had treated him like any other visitor, which made Evan wonder if Natalie had told their son about him yet.

Multicolored building blocks, toy cars and plastic animals had been dumped in the corner of the living room between the unlit fireplace and one of the couches. Aidan connected tiny bricks together, constructing a bridge to go over a figure-eight racetrack. His hair flopped onto his forehead. Focused on his task, he bit the corner of his lip.

The same way Evan did when he was writing paddling articles.

Coach reclined at the other end of the opposite couch with reading glasses on his nose and a dog magazine in his hands, even though he hadn't turned a page in ten minutes. His chest rose and fell rhythmically as gentle snores drifted across the room.

Natalie entered through the arched doorway between the living room and dining room, carrying a plate of chocolate chip cookies, which she set on the coffee table. "You two almost ready to make root beer floats?"

"After I finish my bridge."

She removed the magazine from Coach's hands and draped a cream-colored knitted blanket over him.

Evan slid off the cushion and rested his back against the couch. He picked up a plastic zebra lying on its side next to the racetrack. He turned it over and over in his fingers. "Hey, Aidan, have you been to a zoo?"

Aidan looked up from his construction zone, glanced at his mother, then looked back at Evan and nodded. "Mom took me last year. I rode a pony and got my picture taken inside a gorilla."

"Inside a gorilla, you say?" Evan grinned and shot a look at Nat.

"Uh-huh. Then we rode the merry-go-round. Mom, show him the picture of me inside the gorilla."

"Sure, honey." Natalie crossed the living room to one of the built-in bookcases and removed a thick blue book. She motioned for Evan to follow her.

Evan pushed to his feet and followed her through the dining room and into the gray-and-white kitchen that smelled faintly of vanilla and sugar as if someone had baked recently.

She placed the book on the island and pulled out a counter stool. "Have a seat. Want some coffee?"

He held up a hand. "I'm fine, thanks."

She slid the other stool out, putting a little distance

between them, and picked up the padded book. "I have a confession. I wasn't quite sure how today would go, so I haven't told Aidan who you are yet."

Fighting the frustration welling in his chest, Evan heaved a sigh and raised an eyebrow.

Pink stained Natalie's cheeks as she traced the gold foil around the edge of the cover.

He tried to be patient and understanding and see things from her point of view, but, man, she'd had five years to tell Aidan who his father was. What was she waiting for?

Sure, she needed to protect Aidan, but what did she think Evan was going to do? Take off with him?

She set the book on the counter and pushed it toward him. "This is a scrapbook my aunt made of Aidan's first five years. I want you to have it."

He shot her a surprised look, then opened the cover and stared at the tiny infant with a scrunched-up face wrapped in a blue blanket covered in yellow stars. Even with his eyes closed, the baby's dark hair and the set of his chin reminded Evan of the photograph hanging in the farmhouse living room—a picture of Evan as an infant.

As he turned the plastic-covered pages and took in the assorted images placed on background paper with stickers, his son grew from infancy to toddlerhood and then preschool to how he looked today.

Right before his eyes.

And Evan had missed it all.

A pain he couldn't even begin to describe knifed his chest and twisted, leaving him feeling ragged and wounded.

But he couldn't show it.

Not here.

Not now.

Because he was doing everything he could to make this work out.

He wouldn't give Natalie any reason to keep his son from him.

Forcing himself to breathe, Evan kept turning pages.

Toward the end of the book, he found pictures of Aidan riding a merry-go-round and one of him flashing a toothy grin at the camera as he peered through the facial cutout of a painted gorilla.

Evan closed the book and gripped it, trying to find the right words to say. With emotions raging in his chest, he looked at her. "Why are you showing this to me now, Natalie?"

"I don't know. To try and make amends?" She twisted her fingers together. "What I did was wrong, and I can never make up for that, but this at least gives you a glimpse of his very early years. I'll get more photos printed and share them with you."

Evan opened the book in the middle and stared at an image of his son holding a baby bunny in his arms and grinning at the camera. "I should've had more than a glimpse. I should've been there. You should've told me."

She slid off the stool and paced the kitchen with her arms wrapped around her waist. "You're right, but I can't go back and change the past. All we can do is move forward. I hope you can find some way to forgive me, because if you want to be a part of Aidan's life we need to get along. We won't be fighting in front of him." Her words and her tone left no room for argument.

Evan rested his elbow on the counter and cradled his head in his hand. He didn't want to fight, either.

Somehow, some way, he had to figure out how to forgive Natalie.

For all of their sakes.

Man, it was hard.

He closed the album, rested a hand on top of it and leveled Nat with a direct look. "When do you plan to tell him about me?"

She moved to the sink and stared out the window, her back to him. A moment later she turned with a look of resignation on her face. "Evan, I promise I did not do this to hurt you intentionally. I did try to find you and tell you about Aidan. I went to one of your races. I asked for you."

"You did? When?"

"About a week after I learned I was pregnant. I don't even remember which race it was. Dad had found out where you'd be from Chuck. I booked a one-way flight to Colorado in mid-July, I think. You had just finished a race and were coming out of the water with your paddle held over your head, wearing the face of a victor. People flocked around you, and a woman with blond braids threw her arms around you and kissed you in front of everyone."

Evan scraped a hand over his face as memories of that day came into focus, including the woman he'd never met before kissing him and getting it captured on camera. "I'm sorry, Nat. I never saw you…never knew you were there. Why didn't you say something?"

"I did—well, I tried. I mean, I tried to wait and pull you aside, but I got lost in the shuffle. I didn't want to be one of your groupies. I didn't want that lifestyle of living in a hotel, going from race to race. But it wasn't about what I wanted. You had a right to know about the baby. Once I got home, I tried calling and texting you for two weeks. When you didn't call or message me back, I figured you had moved on—especially after I saw that woman kiss you—and didn't want to hear from me again." Tears glistened in her eyes as her jaw set firm. "I love Aidan more than anything, and I will do what it takes to protect him. Even if it means protecting him from you."

Evan pushed away from the island, strode across the room and stood in front of her. "It must have been around when I dropped my phone in the drink and had to buy a new one as soon as I could make it into town. I lost all my photos, contacts, messages, everything. I went off Dad's family plan and got my own, which included a new phone number."

She folded her arms over her chest. "How do I know you're telling me the truth?"

He lifted his hands. "Why would I lie to you?"

"To save face? To avoid your responsibilities?"

Evan ground his teeth and fought against the words clawing at his throat. "I've always been a man of my word, and you know it, Nat. How do I know that you're the one telling me the truth?"

Natalie gave him another long look, then slowly pulled her phone out of her back pocket. She scrolled through one of the apps, then handed it to him.

He took it and read a long series of one-sided texts asking him to call her. With time stamps that matched her story.

She was telling the truth.

He was the loser father who had abandoned his son. All because he had been horsing around with his team-mates and dropped his phone in the river.

Way to go, knucklehead.

And he'd missed out on the first five years of his son's life.

Handing the phone back to her, Evan softened his tone. "Natalie, I will never ever hurt Aidan, at least not intentionally."

She thrust it back in her pocket. "He needs to know his dad's going to be there for him. I know what it's like to have a father come in and out of your life, leaving behind nothing but a string of empty words and broken promises."

Evan cocked his head and frowned. "What are you talking about? Coach is one of the most stable fathers there is. His words are practically chiseled in stone. When he says something, he means it."

Nat's face paled. Then she closed her eyes and shook her head. "Not Ted. Never mind. Forget it. That's not what I meant."

Evan touched her elbow. "Then tell me. I want to know."

"If we're gonna make this work, you have to promise never to hurt Aidan."

"Of course. You have my word. I've said that already."

Nat's shoulders slumped. "You gave me your word, so now you'll have to show me through your actions. I'll tell Aidan tonight."

"Then what?"

"What do you mean, then what?"

"The kid's bound to have questions. What will you tell him?"

"Well, the truth, of course."

"The real truth…or your version of it?"

As soon as he said the words, Evan wished he could

snatch them back. He didn't want to antagonize Natalie, but his frustrations seemed to slip out before he could stop himself.

At least having Aidan know the truth about Evan was a step in the right direction.

And maybe they could move to some sense of normalcy, whatever that would be.

Chapter Five

"*The real truth...or your version of it?*"

Did Evan really believe she had skewed the truth for the past five years?

His words lingered in her thoughts, poking and prodding the tender wounds that never quite seemed to heal.

He was probably lashing out from hurt. And she didn't blame him. She may have done the same thing.

Like she'd told Evan, she couldn't make up for past mistakes, but she could do better moving forward, and that began by telling Aidan who his father was.

Even though kids were pretty resilient at his age, she hoped this wasn't something he'd throw back in her face when he grew older.

She couldn't worry about that now, though. She needed to follow through with her promise to Evan.

Cheeks still pink from his shower and damp curls plastered to his forehead, Aidan crawled into bed and slid his clean feet under the Spider-Man sheets that had been her brother's at one time. He rested his head on the pillow and pulled the comforter up to his chin. "Will you read me a story?"

"Of course." Natalie sat on the edge of the bed and smoothed his hair off his forehead. He needed a trim soon. "Did you have a fun day today, sweetie?"

He grinned and nodded. "Yep. I helped Grandpa feed the dogs. We played catch with Joey and Chandler—two new dogs at the kennel."

"That sounds like a lot of fun. No wonder Grandpa was so sleepy after dinner." She smoothed out his folded-down top sheet. "So, what did you think of the man who came to visit us tonight?"

Aidan shrugged and gave her a blank look. "Evan? The guy who made you cry?"

"He didn't mean to make me cry. His name is Evan Holland. His family owns a farm with all kinds of animals, including baby cows. Evan's dad is good friends with Grandpa."

Aidan cocked his head and shot her a "you've got to be kidding" look. "Calves, Mom. Baby cows are called calves."

Natalie laughed. "You're absolutely right."

He sat up, his face animated. "Can we see them?"

"Maybe. But I wanted to talk to you about something else. Something important. You know how I tell you it's important to tell the truth?"

Aidan lay back on his side, tucked his hands between his cheek and his pillow, and nodded. "Yup, and I tell the truth even if I'm going to get in trouble. Did you tell a fib to Grandma and Grandpa?"

Natalie laughed. "No, I didn't. But I haven't been very truthful with someone else I love."

"Who?"

Natalie cupped her son's cheek. "You."

"What did you fib to me about?"

"It wasn't quite a fib. But I didn't tell you all the truth."

"About what?"

"Evan—the man who came to visit us after dinner— used to be very good friends with your uncle Ben, who died before you were born. I've known Evan a long time, and at one time, I loved him."

"Love like you love me?"

"Not quite like I love you because I'm your mommy. More like the way Grandma and Grandpa love each other."

Aidan made a face and stuck out his tongue. "Gross. You mean kissy kind of love?"

Natalie laughed. "Yes, kissy kind of love. Evan and I used to love each other very much, but things didn't work out."

"Why not?"

Natalie shrugged. "Sometimes grown-ups don't always make the right choices."

"You and Evan didn't make the right choice?"

"No, if we had, we'd still be together, I'm sure. But that was in the past. We can't change, but we can learn from it and make better choices. No matter what choices I've made, I'm so glad I have you. When you were born, it made me the happiest mommy in the whole wide world."

"What about my daddy? Was he happy, too? Probably not since I don't have one." His little mouth turned down into a frown.

Natalie wanted to crush him to her chest and apologize over and over again for her failures as a mother. Instead, she sat on the edge of the bed and continued playing with his hair. "Well, that's what I wanted to talk to you about. You *do* have a daddy, honey. Evan, the man who came to visit tonight, is your daddy."

His eyes brightened as he sat up again, knocking his favorite stuffed animal—a monkey named Henry—on the floor. "He is? I have a daddy for real?"

"Yes, baby. For real."

"How come I didn't know him before? How come he's not in my baby pictures?"

The questions that would trail after her for the rest of her life…

"When you were born, Evan was far away, and he didn't know about you."

"Why not? Did you think he wouldn't love me?"

"Oh, he would love you three baggies full. But I didn't tell him about you."

There. She'd said it.

Aidan scrunched up his face again and picked up Henry, clutching him to his chest. "Why not?"

"Because sometimes grown-ups make mistakes. And I made a big one. I tried to tell him once, but when I didn't hear back from him, I wasn't sure he was happy about the news that he had a beautiful baby boy. I texted and I called, but he never answered."

"That's rude. Grandma says we need to respond to people even if we don't like what they have to say. We need to use our manners. He didn't use his manners."

"You know, kiddo, I didn't think so at first, either. But tonight I learned that he had lost his phone in the river and had to buy a new one and ended up with a new number. So he wasn't getting my calls or texts. I had you all to myself, and I was the happiest mommy in the whole wide world."

"Does he want to see me now?"

"Yes, when I told him about you, he became the happiest daddy in the whole wide world. He wants to get to know you. He wants to do fun things with you. What do you think about that?"

Aidan frowned and toyed with Henry's bow tie. "What if he doesn't like me? What if he makes me cry like he made you cry?"

Natalie tapped Aidan on the nose. "Who wouldn't like you? You're the most wonderful boy on the whole planet."

"You have to say that because you're my mom. It's in the rules."

Natalie smiled. "I say it because it's true. But Evan likes you already. You don't have to do anything or change anything about yourself—he loves you just as you are."

"How do you know that?"

"He told me. He wants to get to know you and be a good daddy in your life."

"When can I see him again?"

"When do you want to see him again?"

"Can I see him tomorrow? As long as he doesn't make you cry again?"

Natalie bit back a smile. "I'm sure Evan will be more than okay with it. And don't worry. Evan wouldn't do anything to hurt you—or me—on purpose."

She said those words to reassure her son, but a part of Natalie also knew the truth. Evan would move mountains to protect his son.

And maybe that's part of what she was afraid of.

What if he tried to move those mountains to keep her son away from her? She shook her head. No, she wasn't going down that rabbit hole. Evan wasn't the type to hurt her purposefully. Even after what she had done to him.

Maybe she needed to rethink the supervised visitation. Of course Aidan would be safe with his father. Still, Aidan also needed time to get to know Evan within his comfort zone. She couldn't just thrust her son into Evan's world without any precautions in place. She also needed a way to guard her heart, because from the moment she'd laid eyes on Evan all those old buried feelings came rushing back.

And she wasn't sure how to manage them.

Because she couldn't handle getting her heart broken again.

The man was impossible.

How was Natalie supposed to work with Evan when he wouldn't listen to the advice she offered? The advice gleaned from her years of being a dog trainer.

But whatever.

Forcing a smile in place and schooling her tone, Natalie looked at the man who frustrated her more than any other. "I'm just saying if you—"

"Good boy." Standing next to his foster dog, Evan gave Toby another treat and rubbed his head. He looked at Natalie. "I hear you, and I appreciate what you have to say, but I prefer to do it this way."

As much as she wanted to argue that her way was better, she had to let it go.

She lifted her hands and took a step back. "You're the one who wanted to meet up and see how I handle basic commands. I'm simply showing what's worked best for me. Using visual cues before adding in verbal commands is how I do things."

"And I appreciate that. Even though I'm not a certified professional trainer like you, I've spent my life around dogs. Training Toby correctly *is* important, but I also want to give him a few days to get used to River and me. As I'm spending time with him, I'm using the words so he'll get used to hearing them. Then once I begin teaching him the commands, he'll be more familiar."

"If that's what you want to do, that's fine. I started working with Daisy the day I brought her back to my parents' house. Whatever you choose to do, you need to be sure to stay consistent and structured."

"No, Nat. *You* need to be consistent and structured because that's how you live your life. Every dog is different, and I'll keep working with Toby and find out what's best for him."

"Since we need to agree to disagree, maybe we should work independently and meet up only when it comes to Aidan."

"Now you're mad."

She closed her eyes and counted to three before opening them again and addressing him with a smile. "I'm frustrated that you won't listen to me."

"I heard what you were saying."

"Hearing and listening are two different things." Nat glanced at her smartwatch. "Maybe we should call it a day."

"You seem to be in a hurry to get away from me. We're going to be in each other's lives for good, so you might as well get used to having me around." Evan looked at her with serious eyes. "Keeping Aidan from me was far worse than what you perceived I did to you. If I can put that aside to do what's best for our son, then you need to work through your issues with me to make it work as well, because I'm not going anywhere."

Her gaze drifted over his head and landed on Aidan. He was filling the dogs' water dishes with her dad, whose patience as Aidan tried to carry the bowls without sloshing the water too much filled her chest with love and a little sadness.

Sighing, she turned back to Evan, who sat on the ground with Toby. She sat across from him and tucked her feet under her legs. "I'm sorry. I'm frustrated this morning and I took it out on you. You're right. There's more than one way to train. I'll try to be more open-minded with your methods…and with you."

He flashed her a grin, causing her treacherous heart to jump, and reached for her hand, giving it a gentle squeeze. "And I will try to listen more and be more open to what you're suggesting."

She glanced at the long, tanned fingers that were nicked and callused from his years on the river.

"What are you frustrated about?"

His quiet words snagged a tender piece of her soul. She longed to release the pressures in her chest by letting the words tumble out, along with a good cry. But she had to hold it together. People depended on her. Tears pricked the backs of her eyes as she brushed her fingers through the sun-warmed grass.

"What's going on, Nat? You can talk to me."

She eyed him, looked at her father and son once more and then returned her attention to petting Daisy, who had crawled into her lap. "The surgery was supposed to help Dad get better, but he just seems to be more tired than usual. I came home to help run the business, but being here…" She glanced at Evan again. "It's tough. My dad has always been my strength and now he has to depend on me. Running the kennel and training dogs together created a special bond between us. I developed severe anxiety after we came to live with Ted...I mean, after we moved to this house. Dad used the dogs to bring me comfort."

"He certainly has a way with animals...and people."

"The kennel became our special place. With his recent heart attack, it made me realize how precious our time together really is. A lot of things are changing as my parents get older. I need to be here for Mom, Dad and Aidan."

And you.

But she couldn't voice that.

Evan moved over to Natalie and wrapped an arm around her shoulders. He drew her into his embrace, pressing a kiss to her forehead. "I understand what you're going through, Nat. After the tornado, I felt a lot of the same emotions. Anytime you want to talk, I'm here for you. Whatever you need."

She breathed in the scent of soap clinging to his warm skin and longed to rest in the strength he seemed to be offering. But she couldn't allow herself to depend on him again. Even though he mentioned building a house, once his shoulder healed he'd probably be heading back to his paddling life, leaving her to pick up the pieces of her broken heart once again.

He tipped her chin and looked at her with those incredible blue eyes. "What you have with Coach won't be wasted. You can carry on his legacy by using the skills you've learned to offer that same kind of care and comfort to others."

His words, spoken with warmth and tenderness, nearly unshackled her heart.

Would it be so bad to lean on Evan? Even for a short time?

That would mean trusting him. While she longed to unburden her feelings and emotions, a part of her couldn't forget the past and the heartbreak she'd felt when he walked away.

She couldn't risk that again, no matter how much she wanted to believe he wasn't going anywhere.

Evan pushed to his feet once again and held out a hand to her. "Come on, let's take the dogs for a walk. I promise to listen to what you say about loose leash training, too."

Natalie smiled in spite of herself and put her hand in his, allowing him to pull her up. "Let me tell Dad where we're going and grab Aidan so Dad can take a rest. I'll put Daisy in her crate while we're gone so she can take a nap."

Ten minutes later, they walked down the narrow dirt road that cut through the Bishops' property and led into the woods hemmed in by tall trees and thick grasses. Daisies, buttercups and purple sweet peas dipped and waved as they passed. Birds swooped from branch to branch calling one another. Squirrels and chipmunks skittered across the dirt road and raced up the trees.

"It's peaceful. I like to walk the dogs we board back here. It's away from the distractions of walking them in town."

"Want to know a secret?"

Natalie eyed Evan. "Okay…"

He grinned and touched her elbow, then pointed

ahead. "Up ahead where the road veers to the left, instead of following that path, let's go to the right."

Natalie shielded her eyes with her hand to see where he was suggesting they go. "But there's no path."

"Maybe not a beaten one like this, but there used to be a trail—Ben and I made it. And it leads to the farm. I haven't seen the path in years, but let's be a little adventurous. Do you trust me?"

The weight of his question slugged her in the chest. Did she trust him?

Once they reached the spot where the path split, she stopped, eyed the overgrown area and glanced down at her denim shorts and blue flip-flops. "I'm not exactly dressed to go traipsing through a jungle."

Evan raised an eyebrow as his eyes skimmed over her legs. He grinned. "I think you're dressed perfectly fine."

Her cheeks warmed.

"Hey, Aidan. Wanna go on an adventure?"

Aidan stopped and looked at Evan with his familiar scrunched-up face. "An adventure? Where?"

"Through the grass—I want to show you something."

Aidan looked at her and she gave a slight nod. He returned his attention to Evan and shrugged. "Okay."

Evan held out his hand and Aidan took it. No qualms. No reservations. Innocent trust, expecting Evan to have his best interests at heart.

Natalie could take lessons from her son.

She pulled her phone out of the back pocket of her shorts and snapped a picture of father and son walking through the grass, making a path for her to follow. Toby stayed at Evan's side.

She hurried after them. A moment later, the trees opened and gave way to a small clearing and the sounds of babbling water. A worn footbridge stretched across a narrow stream.

Evan unclipped Toby's leash. The dog bolted down the bank and lapped the water.

"Cool!" Aidan dropped Evan's hand and raced toward the bridge.

Evan reached out and caught him by the shirttail. "Hey, buddy. Slow down. That bridge isn't very safe."

Aidan stopped at the edge of the bridge. "Can I cross it?"

"Not until I check it out. It hasn't been used in years. The boards are worn and need to be replaced."

Natalie reached the creek bank and shaded her eyes to look beyond the water. "What's on the other side of the creek?"

"The farm, specifically my property. This is a narrow section of Arrowhead Creek that cuts through our land. Ben and I made the footbridge when we were in middle school so we could get to each other's houses faster."

"How did I not know that?"

"You're not the only one who can keep a secret." Evan kicked one of the uneven boards on the bridge with the toe of his shoe. "We could easily cross without it except during the rainy season when this section of the creek swelled."

Aidan sat on the edge of the bank with his hands behind him. "Mom, can I play in the water?"

"No, honey. That bank's pretty steep, and you can't swim."

"But I can see the bottom. The water's not very deep."

"Not today, Aidan." Her voice firm.

Evan scowled at her. "What do you mean he can't swim? His grandfather's the county swim coach."

Natalie held up her hands in a back-off gesture. "I'm well aware. Aidan's not ready."

Evan glanced at their son, then back to her. "*He's* not? Or *you're* not? You have to loosen the apron strings a little, Nat, and let the kid live."

"What if he gets hurt? What if something happens?"

He took two steps toward her, his back to Aidan, and reached for her hands. "You are not in this alone anymore. I'm here to help both of you. Between Coach and me, we can teach him to swim. Water is in the kid's veins, remember, Ms. State Champion?"

She shook her head and stared at her toes, trying not to think about how Evan's touch made her feel. "That was a lifetime ago. But you're right—he does need to learn. Maybe once Dad is allowed to go back to work."

"I can teach him."

"What about your shoulder?"

"My sling comes off in a few days. I'll start physical therapy, and I'll be as good as new."

And heading back to his first love—the river—and leaving them behind.

Natalie forced a smile, thankful her sunglasses hid the sudden wash of moisture across her eyes. "We'll see."

Stepping away from Evan, she crossed the grass to sit next to Aidan. Better to get in the habit now of keeping her distance from the man whose presence scrambled her insides rather than fall in love with him all over again and pick up the pieces later.

Or was she too late?

In the short time Evan had been back in Shelby Lake, he'd taken up residence once again in her thoughts and dreams. Part of her wanted more, and another part was too afraid to invest because she knew what would happen when he walked away.

Chapter Six

Evan was a failure as a father.

Somehow, he needed to help Aidan calm down. All of his tactics had failed. Beyond seeing his twin niece and nephew while home, and hanging out with his team-mates' kids, he didn't have much experience with children.

How did other parents manage meltdowns?

He glanced at his sport smartwatch. Seven minutes and four seconds.

That was how long Aidan had been screaming since he woke up to use the bathroom and found Evan instead of his mother in the living room.

When Nat called an hour ago and asked him to come and stay with Aidan while she drove her parents to the ER, Evan didn't even hesitate. He'd jumped in his truck and headed over the hill.

Apparently, Coach had gotten dizzy, fallen and cut his head on the bathroom counter. After Evan helped load him into Nat's SUV, he'd cleaned up the counter and floor.

Then Aidan woke up, which spiraled into a meltdown.

Evan reached for the kid curled up in a ball on the floor between the couch and wall. "Hey, buddy. Let's watch *Daniel Tiger*."

Livie and Landon loved *Daniel Tiger*, the animated show that had followed in *Mister Rogers*'s footsteps.

Aidan slapped at Evan's hand. "No! I hate *Daniel Tiger*! I want my mom."

"Your mom will be back in a little while." Evan eyed his watch one more time.

Eight minutes.

"Where is she?" He sniffed and wiped his nose on the hem of his shirt.

"I told you—she had to run an errand with your grandma and grandpa."

"I wanna go, too." Fresh tears trailed down his face and dripped off his chin.

"I'm sorry, buddy, but you can't. Your mom will be back soon. For now, you're here with me."

"I don't like you." Aidan scrambled to his feet, raced to the front door and threw it open.

Evan tried not to let the words spoken in fear and frustration jab him in the throat.

Less than two steps behind him, he wrapped his arm around the boy's waist and hauled him back before Aidan could escape barefoot into the dark.

Alice, the Bishops' collie, barked, jumped off the couch and pranced around them. Barking sounded from down the hall—Daisy, crated in Nat's bedroom.

Great. Let's get everyone wound up.

Aidan tried to wriggle out of his grasp and pounded his small fists against Evan's chest and neck.

Careful not to trip over Alice, Evan carried him back

to the couch, trying to ignore the fire igniting in his shoulder, and sat, cradling his son against his chest.

His son who wanted nothing to do with him.

Evan tried to remember how his brother Tucker handled his twins' fits, but he was drawing a blank.

Wait a minute—what was that ridiculous song Mom used to sing to them before bed when they were kids?

Evan hummed a few bars of the tune from his childhood as it started coming back to him. He sang about going to the animal fair with baboons combing hair and sneezing elephants.

Aidan's rigid body relaxed in Evan's arms.

He sang about a monkey next to a skunk, and Aidan giggled. Evan stilled a moment and then launched into the song a third time with more gusto and exaggeration, creating his own words that didn't seem to make sense.

By the time he started at the beginning once again, Aidan pushed away from his chest and sang along with him.

Still holding the child in his arms, Evan brushed Aidan's hair off his forehead and thumbed away stray tears from his cheeks.

"Are you really my dad?" Aidan looked at him with questioning eyes.

"Yes, I am." Evan looked down at the child's sweet and innocent face.

"Okay." Aidan sighed and shifted in Evan's arms, resting the back of his head against Evan's chest. He rubbed his tired-looking eyes and smothered a yawn. "Can I watch *Daniel Tiger* now?"

So much for not liking it.

"Of course." Evan leaned forward, picked up the remote and flipped to the home page that listed the streaming channels. Clicking on one, he scrolled until he found the show Aidan wanted.

Once the yellow-and-brown-striped tiger wearing a red sweater started singing, Aidan relaxed in his arms. Within minutes, he was snoring softly.

Evan shifted into a more comfortable position and settled back against the throw pillow, his arms wrapped around his son. Alice jumped up next to them and rested by Evan's hip, her paws tucked under her muzzle as she watched them.

He exhaled slowly.

He'd done it.

He'd managed to quiet his son's screams with a silly song. He should carry him to his bed where he could sleep comfortably. And he would. In a minute, maybe. For now, though, he had five years to make up for.

Evan adjusted Aidan in his arms and closed his eyes for a moment.

A hand touched his shoulder.

Evan's eyes shot open to find Natalie standing over him, looking tired and something else he couldn't quite describe. Anxious, maybe?

"Hey, sleepyheads."

Her gentle tone stirred something deep in his chest. He smiled and rubbed his eyes with his thumb and forefinger.

As he tried to shift Aidan's weight, a flare of pain spiked through his shoulder. He sucked in a sharp breath.

Nat reached over to remove Aidan from his arms, her fingers grazing across his chest.

Aidan's eyes fluttered. "Mommy."

"Hi, baby." Her quiet whisper brought a smile to Aidan's face.

"You came back."

"Of course. I will always come back to you."

"Good." He closed his eyes as she carried him down the hall.

Evan stood, scrubbed a hand over his face, then smoothed down his hair. He winced as his shoulder tightened. He straightened the pillows and folded a knitted afghan he had tossed over Aidan.

Nat returned to the living room and smothered a yawn. "Thanks for coming at the last minute."

"Of course. How's Coach?"

"He ended up with four stitches, and they're keeping him overnight for observation for a mild concussion and a possible reaction to a new medication his cardiologist added recently. It could explain the fatigue and lack of energy he's been experiencing lately. Mom decided to stay at the hospital with him." Her voice caught and she pressed a fist to her mouth.

"Come here." Evan wrapped an arm around her and drew her to his chest. He pressed a kiss to her forehead. "What can I do to help?"

"You're doing it now." Her words were muffled against the fabric of his T-shirt. "Dad asked if Ben was meeting us at the hospital. That's when Mom became more concerned."

Evan lifted a hand to brush her hair off her face. "I'm sorry, Nat."

She cupped her hand over his and gave it a gentle squeeze. "Thanks. I'm sorry Aidan woke up. I figured he would have stayed asleep. How was he?"

"He freaked out when he realized you weren't here. But we handled it, and he fell back to sleep."

"I hope he wasn't too much for you. He can be a little difficult at times."

"Nothing I couldn't handle."

"How's the shoulder?" She ran a gentle hand over his sling.

On fire.

He shrugged. "It's fine. I should get out of here so you can get some sleep."

The last thing he wanted to do was leave, but it was the right thing all around.

Nat stepped out of his arms and reached for a tissue from the box on the coffee table between the matching couches. She wiped her eyes, wadded it up and stuffed it in her front pocket. She walked him to the door. "Thanks again, Evan."

"Anytime." He wanted to lean over and kiss her. Instead, he gave her a wave and stepped into the darkness.

After opening the truck door, Evan slid behind the steering wheel and leaned his head against the headrest.

He might not be Father of the Year, have Tuck's parenting skills or even his father's wisdom, but he had managed time alone with his son without any permanent damage.

Maybe there was hope for them after all.

He knew one thing, though—he wasn't about to give up trying.

After helping Natalie out the other night by caring for Aidan, Evan needed to learn how to connect with his son.

Now that Coach had been home from the hospital for a couple of days, maybe having lunch together would give them a chance to catch up. And maybe his former mentor could give him some parenting tips.

Evan pushed through the smoky glass door at Joe's Diner, pocketed his keys and tucked his sunglasses onto the neck of his royal blue T-shirt. He scanned the busy dining room to see if Coach had arrived.

He'd offered to pick him up, but Coach said the walk to the diner would be good for him.

Scents of grilled meat and salty french fries shot straight to Evan's gut, making his mouth water.

Spying an empty booth, he passed the counter, waved to Isabella, his brother's fiancée, and snagged an empty booth that overlooked the parking lot.

He read the place mat menu, even though he had his order ready in his head before he stepped inside. A lot of changes had happened since Isabella had returned to town to help save her father's place.

"Evan Holland, why are you wasting time with that menu when we both know you're going to order the same thing you always do?"

Evan looked up from the menu and grinned. "Noel, how are you doing?"

He stood and hugged the petite fortysomething server holding a full pot of coffee and a whole lotta sass.

She set the pot on the table and wrapped her arms around his neck. One of her auburn corkscrew curls escaped from her ponytail and tickled his chin. "Look at you with that sun-kissed, wild hair."

He smoothed a hand over the waves that seemed to have a mind of their own. "Wild? You should've seen it before I cut it."

She batted at his chest and shot him a flirtatious

smile. "Positively dashing. So, what brings you back home?"

Evan jerked his head toward his shoulder, finally free of the sling. "Took a dunk in the drink and ended up having surgery."

"Ouch. I hope it heals quickly, so you can get back on the water before the season ends."

Not likely. But he appreciated her optimism.

"Thanks, we'll see."

"So, the usual?" She pulled her order pad out of her apron pocket.

He grinned. "Am I that predictable?"

"Bacon cheeseburger and garbage fries? Nah, you're just a man who knows what he likes."

An image of Natalie dashed through his thoughts, but he tucked it away.

"Actually, I'm meeting Coach Bishop for lunch. I'll have an iced tea, then wait until he arrives to order, if that's okay?"

"Absolutely, sugar." She reached for her pot and returned to the service station.

Resting his elbow on the table, Evan cupped his chin in his hand and stared out the window, trying not to let Noel's hope discourage him.

A week ago, he would have done almost anything to get back on the water, especially now that his sling was off and he'd be starting physical therapy soon.

But now…

Now he had a son.

And Nat.

Although he had a greater chance at winning over his son than the boy's mother.

"Now there's a man in thought."

He jolted and turned to find Coach standing at the booth. Evan jumped to his feet and wrapped Coach in a quick one-armed hug. "Coach. Thanks for meeting me. How are you doing, man?"

His former mentor and father figure lifted a shoulder, looking tired and drawn. "Hanging in there. Trying to appreciate the care and concern from my hovering wife and daughter. I'm a blessed man, but I must say I'm getting tired of baked chicken and steamed broccoli."

"Lunch is on me, so get whatever you'd like."

"That's not necessary."

"I invited you. I'm paying."

"Well, thank you."

As Coach studied the place mat menu, Evan took in the man's thin frame and graying hair. Coach had never been a beefy man, and years of swimming created lean muscle and a youthful appearance. But the heart attack seemed to have taken a lot out of him.

"Dr. Mary and Nat have your best interests at heart."

"Maybe so. Doesn't mean I have to like it." The older man winked at him.

Noel returned and took their order. She came back a moment later with a glass of iced tea for Coach.

After she left, Coach leaned back in the booth. "So what's on your mind, son?"

"What do you mean?"

"As flattered as I am, I doubt you asked me to lunch to shoot the breeze."

Evan scrubbed a hand over his face. Coach had always had the ability to see through him. "It's Aidan. I want to be a good dad. Someday, a great dad. Like mine. Like the way you are with Nat. But he wants nothing to do with me. When Mary and Nat took you for stitches the other night, he woke up and cried for what seemed like an hour before I could even calm him down."

Coach looked at him a moment, then reached into his back pocket and pulled out his wallet. He removed a small stack of photos and thumbed through them. Then he tossed one across the table.

Evan picked it up and stared at a faded image of himself around Aidan's age. Dressed in red swim trunks that came nearly to his knobby knees, he stood on the edge of the pool with his arms wrapped around his waist and tears running down his face.

Evan remembered the day as if it had been yesterday.

"My first swim class. I was terrified. You stood in the water and tried to coax me to get in. Where'd you get this picture?"

"Your mom stood in the doorway of the locker room and snapped it. After she had gotten it developed, she showed it to me, and I asked if I could have it."

"Why?"

"Because that day, I saw something in you. I knew you were going to be special. And I wanted proof to offer you someday." Coach seared him with a look that had motivated Evan over the years—a look of pride.

Evan broke eye contact with the man and stared at the words on the place mat. "I think your heart attack has messed with your brain, old man."

"Oh, no doubt about that, kid, but I was right."

"I'm nobody special." He forced the words past the dryness in his throat.

"Says you."

Evan fingered the photo once again before tossing it across the table. "What does this have to do with Aidan?"

"Remember how scared you were? I tried to get you to come into the pool and your screams echoed off the walls. You were afraid. You didn't know me. But your mom refused to let you quit. Twice a week, she brought you to me kicking and screaming. One day you tried to get away and ended up falling into the pool."

Evan cupped a hand over his face as the memory surged to the forefront of his thoughts. "I tried to get to the ladder and kept going under. You reached for me and spoke so calmly."

"Remember what I said?"

"The hard part's over—you got in the water."

"Exactly. Aidan's a sweet kid and he will come around. The hard part's over—you showed up. Just keep coming around, spend quality time with him, and he'll warm up to you." Coach leaned forward and flicked his eyes over the dining room. Then he brought a hand to the side of his face. "You didn't hear this from me, and if you say so, I'll deny it, but the kid has a sweet spot for grape freeze pops. The kind in the plastic tube. He likes how they make his tongue purple."

Evan raised an eyebrow. "So you're suggesting I bribe him to like me?"

Coach lifted his shoulders and laughed. "Hey, whatever works, right?"

Evan wound a straw wrapper around his finger as his gaze shifted to the parking lot. "Why didn't she tell me? I would have been there for her every step of the way."

"I know you would have, son. Natalie Grace has a lot of fears, but I don't have to tell you. After her dad walked out on her for the last time—"

Evan jerked his gaze back to Coach and frowned. "Wait, what? You walked out on her? When?"

"What? Of course not." Then, almost as if he realized what he'd said, Coach paled and covered his face with his hand. "Oh, this new medicine. Doc said there'd be some confusion. Headaches, too." He slid out of the booth. "Sorry, son, but I'm not feeling so well. I need to go."

Evan reached for his wallet. "Let me leave money for the check, and I'll take you home."

"No need, a walk will do me good." Without another word he headed for the door.

Evan hurried after Coach to get him to reconsider, but when he realized the man was already out of view, he headed back inside so Noel didn't think he was skipping out without paying.

Back at the table, he picked up the photo Coach had left behind. With the exception of the faded background, he could have been staring at an image of his son.

Noel returned to the table with two plates and set the burgers and fries on the table. "Where'd Coach run off to?"

Evan snitched a fry. "He wasn't feeling well. Sorry to be a pain, but would you mind boxing these up and bringing me the check?"

"Of course, sugar." She headed back to the kitchen and returned a few minutes later with a white bulging take-out bag.

After paying and leaving a generous tip, Evan headed for his truck. Inside, he flicked on the AC and allowed the cold to chill the sauna-like interior. He backed out of the lot and headed for the Bishops' place.

As he pulled into the driveway, Nat disappeared into the kennel.

Evan cut the engine, grabbed Coach's meal and headed for the kennels. As he entered the building, Nat came out of one of the suites, cradling a small dog in her arms. Startled, she looked at him with wide eyes, then her gaze darted around the kennel as if looking for some sort of escape.

Evan lifted a hand. "Hey, Nat."

"Evan. What's up?"

He lifted the bag. "Coach and I were in the middle of lunch, then he split. Is he here?"

"What do you mean he split? That doesn't sound like Dad. Especially when it comes to sneaking one of Joe's burgers. What happened?"

Evan shrugged, replaying their conversation in his head. "I don't really know. We were talking about my first swimming experience, getting to know Aidan better, and then…well, you."

Nat set the dog back in the kennel and closed the door. She wrapped her arms around her waist. "Me? What about me?"

"I asked Coach why you didn't tell me about Aidan. Almost rhetorical, you know. He mentioned you having trust issues after…" Evan dragged a hand over his face and blew out a breath. "After your dad walked out on you for the final time. I asked what he was talking about, and he muttered something about his new medication causing confusion and headaches. He said he didn't feel well and left. That's not like him."

Natalie stared at him with the same deer-in-the-headlights look Coach had given him.

Evan took a step toward her. "What's going on, Nat? What's Ted talking about? Did he walk out on you?"

She looked away and laughed, an almost shrill sound that lacked warmth and humor. "Of course not. Dad's memory hasn't been the same since his heart attack. He's confused like he said. That's all."

Evan eyed her. If Coach's so-called gaffe was confusion, why did Natalie look like a trapped bird? He reached for her hand, but she took a step back. "I don't believe you. What's going on?"

Her shoulders slumped and she lowered her chin. When she raised her head, sadness rimmed her eyes. "Nothing, Evan. Let it go. Please."

He looked at her a moment, then jammed his fists in his front pocket and ground his jaw. "Why won't you talk to me?"

"You're creating something out of nothing."

"If that were true, then you and Coach wouldn't be acting so weird."

"Maybe you're the one being weird."

He strode back to the door and picked up the bag, removing Coach's take-out container and setting it on the desk. "Here's his lunch." He started for the door, then turned back to Natalie. "I don't know why I keep trying when you've made it perfectly clear you plan to keep me at arm's length."

"Evan…" She took a step toward him.

"Forget it, Nat. I'm sorry I bothered you." He headed out the door and forced himself not to slam it behind him. No sense in upsetting the dogs over his frustration with Natalie shutting him out. Again.

He was such a fool.

When was he going to learn she wanted nothing to do with him?

If it wasn't for Aidan, he'd get in his truck and keep driving. No, he wasn't going to be that guy. He didn't walk away from his responsibilities.

But, man, Natalie wasn't making it easy for him.

Chapter Seven

What was wrong with her?

Why did she turn into a jerk every time Evan was around?

The concern on his face when he'd asked about what her father had said over their lunch was nearly her undoing. She had always admired Evan's compassion although, apparently, she didn't trust him enough to share what was bothering her.

Sitting in the kennel office with her head bent over a stack of applications for a kennel technician, Natalie leafed through the papers, seeing the words without reading them.

Deciding she needed a break and maybe another cup of coffee, Natalie pushed away from the desk and turned. Then jumped. Mom stood in the doorway with her arms folded over her chest and leaned against the doorjamb.

"You startled me." Natalie pressed a shaky hand against her pounding heart.

Mom pushed away from the door and walked over to Natalie. "Sorry about that. It wasn't my intention. You looked deep in thought and I didn't want to break your concentration."

Natalie eyed her mother's cute blue flowered skirt, white T-shirt and brown leather flats. With her hair pulled back in a low ponytail, she could have passed for one of her interns. As well, she looked more like she was just beginning her morning shift rather than ending it.

After Dad's heart attack, Mom had cut back her own hours, allowing Willow to take over the afternoons. That gave her mother more time to be with him.

"I had finished my appointments and paperwork when Ted came into my office very upset. He'd planned to have lunch with Evan, but in the course of their conversation, he inadvertently mentioned Brady. He went into the house to lie down."

Natalie waved away her mother's words and shook her head. "I'm sorry Dad got upset and ended his lunch with Evan so abruptly. He didn't do it on purpose. As you keep telling me—it's in the past, right?"

"If that's the case, why are you still so fearful about telling Evan about him? Or even letting Evan get close to you. He's a good man with a sincere heart."

"A sincere heart is great, but he's not rooted. He travels from one river to the next, living in an RV."

"He's following his passion. That doesn't change his character. And maybe he just needs a good reason to settle down."

"He had a good reason once—me. But his passion for paddling was stronger. I let him go. No strings." Tears pricked the backs of her eyes as she replayed the final argument that had destroyed everything between them.

"Oh, honey, but there were strings. You wanted everything on your terms. And you didn't let him go—

you pushed him away, lashing out and blaming him for Ben's death when the real issue was you being afraid he was going to break his promises and abandon you the same way Brady did."

"Why do you keep bringing up *that* man?" Natalie couldn't stop the shiver that trailed down her spine.

"He can't hurt you anymore, Natalie."

"I know, Mom. I do. But I still have nightmares about the threats he screamed at you when they arrested him."

"Brady never kept a promise in his life. He's not going to come after us. It would take too much work to find us."

"He betrayed us, left us hungry and homeless and with nothing. I know Evan's nothing like him, but I have to think of Aidan now. I need to focus on helping Dad until he can return to coaching and managing the kennels without me. Then I need to build up my dog training business in Shelby Lake so I can give Aidan a secure future. Evan is all about honesty and integrity. If I tell him about the lie I've been carrying all these years, he's going to get mad again and walk away. Or worse, he'll try to take Aidan, too. So I can't risk that."

"Sweetheart, you've taken a childhood trauma and blown it up into some sort of phobia that controls your life. You can't live constantly looking over your shoulder."

"I know that, but I don't know how to stop it. With his armed robbery and arrest making national news, if someone discovers our connection to him, we could have reporters camped outside our house. We could lose everything all over again. Do you really want that to happen?"

"Of course not. That's why we moved across the

country. That's why we changed our names. We are safe, Natalie." Mom cupped her chin. "We've built a new life in Shelby Lake, and nothing from our past will change that. Trust God. Give this turmoil over to Him, and allow your faith to be greater than your fear."

"I still have nightmares, but this time, my fath— Brady comes after Aidan."

"Oh, honey, what does your therapist say?"

"I haven't seen her since I've been back in Shelby Lake."

"Then let's find a local one."

The idea of starting all over again with a new therapist widened the pit in Natalie's stomach. Why couldn't she be normal for once and just focus on what was in front of her instead of the terrors that crept through her sleep? Life would be so much simpler.

"Maybe. I'll think about it."

"Natalie, I just want you to live your best life."

"I'm not even sure what that looks like, Mom."

"What do you want?"

"Security."

"And what does that look like to you?"

Natalie shrugged. "Roots. A stable home. A family with someone who can love me—the real me, fears and all. Peace, and the ability to look to the future without waiting for the other shoe to drop."

"I want those things for you, too, honey. And for Aidan. You don't think you could have them with Evan?"

She lifted a shoulder. "Evan has wanderlust. I want a permanent address."

"There's more to life than where you live."

"How can we put down roots if Evan is racing down

rivers and going from one event to the next? I saw him in action. I saw the adrenaline rush. The winner's high…"

"And it reminded you of your father." Mom's quiet words pinched her chest.

She nodded slowly as faded images from the past flickered through her head. She tried to blink them away but they remained as if someone hit the pause button. "Brady would win big and it fueled his addiction, even though he promised to stop, to change. But he didn't and it cost us everything."

She had learned to fear those nights when he lost and took his frustration out on them.

"I've known Evan for over twenty years, and he is nothing like Brady. Evan is good and kind and understands loss. Give him a chance—he could give you everything you've always wanted." Her mother's words jerked her back to the present.

"Except his forgiveness. He's already said what I've done was unforgivable."

"He was talking through his broken heart."

"How do you do it, Mom?"

"Do what?"

"Keep your faith greater than your fear."

"It isn't always easy, but God promises to never leave us or forsake us."

"Where was He when we lost everything?"

"Working to give us an even better future. He brought Ted into our lives. Without his support and encouragement, I couldn't have finished my education to become a vet. He helped set up my practice. He adopted you and Ben once I terminated Brady's parental rights for abandonment after his incarceration. Ted's been the kind of father both of you needed. And a wonderful grandfather to Aidan. His faith keeps me going when mine wavers."

"And we almost lost him."

"But we didn't. So mark that in the praise column. Ted's heart attack was a wake-up call to make better choices. For all of us. We can't live in fear of the future, honey. Give your fears over to God and watch Him give you everything your heart desires."

Natalie longed for the peace that radiated off her mother. Yes, she wanted those things, but how did she even stop being fearful enough to take that first step of faith?

For the first time since leaving home to chase his paddling dreams, Evan was about to do something he hadn't ever considered—put down roots.

It was time, and now he had more than himself to think about.

His recent physical therapy appointments had been discouraging—he wasn't gaining the range of motion he needed to endure heavy paddling on the water.

Somehow, he needed to figure out what to do with the rest of his life.

In the meantime, he could put down roots to show Natalie he was more than capable of caring for their son.

Aidan needed more than a table that converted into a bed to sleep on. The Water Wagon had been just fine for a bunch of River Rats. Once his house was in place, he'd give the RV to his teammates for them to use as they furthered their water adventures. Without him.

After a week of hard work that did little to promote healing in his shoulder, Evan's land was going to have a house, or rather it would once the permits were approved and the prefabricated home he had purchased was delivered and set up.

Thanks to his brothers' and his dad's help, they'd managed to get the foundation dug and ready for the concrete to be poured.

His gut had the same roller-coaster feeling he dealt with before every race.

Maybe this would help ease Nat's fears about him taking off. He wasn't going anywhere. Sure, his bum shoulder pretty much guaranteed he wasn't going to paddle again anyway. Still, that wouldn't be enough for a mom who wore fear like a thick coat.

And that's why Evan asked her and Aidan to meet him on Holland Hill.

As if on cue, her SUV crested the hill, the midafternoon sun glinting off the metallic paint on the hood, and pulled in beside his truck. She stepped out and the sunlight haloed her hair. She opened the back door, and a moment later Aidan scrambled out.

He rounded the front of Evan's truck and stopped. He looked at Evan, dropped his gaze to his feet and lifted his hand in a small wave. "Hi, Ev...I mean, Dad."

Evan's heart crashed against his ribs. He swallowed past the sudden thickening in his throat and grinned, ruffling Aidan's hair. "Hey, buddy."

Progress. And Evan would take it.

Aidan dropped to the ground between River and Toby and wrapped an arm over each of them.

River licked Aidan's cheek, causing him to giggle and wipe at his face. Toby nuzzled his nose under Aidan's hand for the petting to continue.

Nat appeared, holding on to Daisy's leash. Her hair had been gathered in a ponytail and looped through a navy Bishop Boarding & Kennels baseball hat. She wore a blue T-shirt and tan shorts that exposed toned legs. Sunglasses shaded her eyes, and she smiled. "Hi."

His pulse picked up speed. "Hey. Glad you could make it."

"What's going on? Doing some farm construction?" She eyed the foundation.

"Not exactly." Evan waved a hand over the expanse of the land. "This is my property. And that—" he pointed to the deep trenches "—is where my new house will sit. Jake, Tucker, Dad and I have been working on getting the foundation ready. Once my permits are approved, I'll have the basement foundation poured. After that, a company will install a prefabricated house."

"Like the ones you showed me in the brochure?"

"Yes, exactly. The house is built in sections and then loaded on trucks. They bring them out, set the sections in place and then finish assembling the house."

"What about things like water and sewage and electricity?"

"I've hired a contractor who will come out and take care of all of that. Would you like to see the house I chose?"

"See it how?"

Evan opened the door to his truck and pulled a booklet off the front seat. Leaning against the front bumper, he flipped through the catalog until he found his model home. "This is called Lakewood. Check out the covered wraparound porch. As you enter the house, you walk into the foyer. If you turn right, you'll enter a large living room with vaulted ceilings and a stone fireplace. The open kitchen and dining area are to the left. Upstairs, there's a loft for an office, a library, or maybe even a play space. Down the hall, we'll have three bedrooms, including the master bedroom with an en suite bathroom."

Evan looked at Aidan. "Hey, buddy, how would you like to pick out your own bedroom?"

"Really?" Aidan jumped to his feet and pulled down the brochure to peer over it.

"Yes, really."

"Cool! I want a superhero bedroom."

"Which superhero?"

He spread his arms out wide. "All of them. Superheroes help me to be brave and strong."

Evan tapped Aidan's chest gently. "You're strong and brave already. Courage comes from within."

"What's courage?"

"Courage is knowing something makes you afraid, but you do it anyway."

"Do you have courage?" Aidan looked at him with an earnest expression.

"I try to. It's okay to be afraid—we just don't want to let those fears keep us from living our lives." Evan kept his gaze steady on Aidan so his eyes didn't dart in Nat's direction.

"Do you ever get scared?"

"We all get scared. Even grown-ups." Evan lifted his left arm. "A little while ago, I was paddling down the river in my kayak, going superfast. I took my eyes off the water and looked behind me to see how far behind the other guy was. I should have paid attention to what I was doing."

"What happened?"

"I didn't see a downed tree. If I had been paying attention to the water, I could have avoided it."

"Did you crash?"

"Yep. Big-time. I made a mistake and ended up flipping my kayak and smashing my shoulder on a big rock under the water."

"Ouch. Did it hurt?"

"It hurt like you wouldn't believe."

"Did you cry?"

"No, but I wanted to. Because of the way my kayak landed upside down, I was trapped underneath and my foot was caught in the downed tree."

"That would scare me."

"It did scare me. Then I remembered a time when my brothers and I had built a fort in the hay bales. Later, we decided to play hide-and-seek. I hid in the hay fort, but while waiting for them to find me, the fort collapsed."

"Were you scared?"

"Yes, I was. I had to push my way out. After I flipped my kayak, I remembered that time in the hay fort. And how I got out. That's what I did with my kayak. I pushed it up enough so I could get my head out of the water and breathe."

"Then what happened?"

"My teammates had to rescue me. But I lost the practice race."

Aidan threw himself at Evan. "I'm sorry you got hurt and lost the race. I'm glad you're okay."

Evan gripped the boy to his chest. "It's okay, because I came home and found you. You're the best prize of all. Better than any trophy. Just remember—we don't know how brave we actually are until we need to be."

"You're like a superhero—strong and brave. I'm glad you're my dad."

Evan's throat tightened. "I'm so glad you're my Aidan."

"Can I paint my room any color I want?"

"Sure can. We can go to the paint store this week to get some color samples. I'll give them to the home building guys."

Aidan shook his head and popped out his bottom lip. He looked down at his feet and dug the toe of his sneaker into the dirt. Then he raised his face to Evan. "But I wanted to do it together. You and me. And Mom."

Evan cupped his son's chin. "Deal. We'll do it together."

Aidan grinned and turned to Nat. "You hear that, Mom? We get to do it together."

Nat pasted a smile in place, but the look in her eyes showed something other than excitement.

Too bad.

Evan had five years to make up for, and if his son wanted to paint his room as a family, then they would.

Aidan grabbed Natalie's hand. "Mom, what color will you paint your room?"

Natalie's eyes widened as she looked at Evan.

He smothered a smile.

Natalie knelt in front of Aidan and reached for his hands. "Honey, I won't have a room at Daddy's new house."

"But when Dad gets his new house, we'll live there together, right? Since you're my mom and he's my dad. Moms and dads live together like Grandma and Grandpa."

"Grandma and Grandpa are married, and that's why they live together. Your dad and I aren't married, so we will live in different houses. But that doesn't change how much we love you. It just means you get two bedrooms instead of one."

Aidan's face scrunched as he processed the information, then he looked up and threw out his hands. "I got it—you and Dad can get married like Grandma and Grandpa, then we'll all move into the new house when it's put together. We can paint my room, then your room. Like a family."

Evan's chest pinched.

If only…

Natalie stood and shoved her fingers into the front pocket of her shorts. "I wish it could be that simple, Aidan, but it's not."

"Why not?"

Natalie shot Evan a pleading look.

"Hey, buddy. Every family is different. Sometimes moms and dads live together and sometimes they don't. Even though we don't live together, that doesn't change how we feel about you."

"But I want us to be a family with one house, not two."

He got it. He did. And truth be told, at one time Evan had wanted the same thing.

But their lives were different now.

He and Nat were different.

When he married, he wanted a wife who could trust him with her deepest fears and secrets—someone who could trust him with her whole heart.

And that wasn't Natalie.

As much as he wanted to make his son's wish come true, they had too many obstacles to overcome before they could be the family that Aidan wanted.

Chapter Eight

Was it too late to back out?

Even though Evan had told her repeatedly she had nothing to fear from his family, her nerves had a python grip around her stomach as she pulled into Chuck and Claudia Holland's driveway.

Chuck was one of her father's closest friends, and she'd been to the Holland farm hundreds of times growing up.

This time was different.

She'd kept Aidan from them for the past five years. She wouldn't blame them for hating her. Maybe coming to the farm was a mistake after all.

Of course, Evan had invited them to visit in front of Aidan after they viewed his property yesterday. How could she say no when Aidan seemed so excited about it?

She parked the car and shut off the engine. Not hearing anything from Aidan, she glanced in the rearview mirror to find him sound asleep with his head lolling forward and his hand on Daisy's head.

The front door to the farmhouse opened. Evan stepped out dressed in gray shorts and a red T-shirt advertising some paddling company. The shirt hugged his chest and strong shoulders. He lifted a hand, jogged down the front steps and rounded the car to open her door.

"I'm glad you came. I half expected to get a text that you couldn't make it."

Without a word, Natalie unplugged her phone from the charging cord and held it out to him, showing an open texting window with the unsent apology she had typed.

The corner of his mouth lifted as he read it before handing the phone back to her. "But you came anyway. Thanks."

Her skin flushed from his tender tone. She stowed the phone in the back pocket of her jeans and pulled her keys out of the ignition, dropping them on the console. She didn't have to worry about anyone taking her car on the farm.

Sliding out from behind the wheel, she straightened next to Evan. Even though he was a head taller, their eyes connected.

For a moment, she forgot her fears.

"Mom. We there yet?" Aidan stirred in the back seat and rubbed an eye with his fist.

"Yes, we are. Time to wake up." Natalie reached in and unbuckled the seat belt that secured his booster seat. "There you go, little man."

He scampered out of the car, then stopped in the driveway. He wrinkled his nose and waved a hand in front of his face. "Pee-ew. Something stinks."

Evan laughed, the rich timbre of his voice causing Natalie's pulse to jump. "Welcome to the farm, Aidan. Would you like to meet my dad and brothers—your other grandparents and uncles?"

Aidan's eyes widened, then he lowered his gaze to his feet. "What if they don't like me?"

Evan shot a glance at Natalie and crouched in front of his son. "Hey, that's impossible. My dad loves everyone, but he will especially love you."

"Why?"

"Because you are family." Evan stood and held out his hand. "Come on. Let's go find him so I can prove how right I am."

Aidan looked at him a moment, then cocked his head and tapped a finger to his chin. He nodded. "Okay, let's do it."

Hand in hand, father and son walked around the side of the house with Natalie right behind them. Her feet felt as if they were chiseled out of concrete.

Evan's family were seated on colorful Adirondack chairs around a stone firepit in the backyard behind the farmhouse. Rows of apple trees surrounded the backyard and separated the living space from the back barnyard. Laughter rose with spirals of smoke.

The knot in Natalie's stomach tightened. She balled her hands into fists and steeled her spine.

She had messed up—big-time—and deserved their wrath. She could handle what they threw her way, but the minute they turned on Aidan, she was out of there and taking her son with her.

"Hey, guys." Evan still held on to Aidan's hand as he approached his family. "This is Aidan. My son."

The pride in his voice and the smile on Evan's face radiated enough energy to power the hilltop. He turned and extended a hand out to Natalie. She took it this once, needing his strength.

Why had she agreed to this?

FREE BOOKS GIVEAWAY

2 FREE ROMANCE BOOKS!

2 FREE SUSPENSE BOOKS!

GET UP TO FOUR FREE BOOKS & TWO FREE GIFTS WORTH OVER $20!

We pay for everything!

YOU pick your books –
WE pay for everything.
You get up to FOUR New Books and TWO Mystery Gifts...absolutely FREE

Dear Reader,

I am writing to announce the launch of a huge **FREE BOOKS GIVEAWAY**... and to let you know that YOU are entitled to choose up to FOUR fantastic books that WE pay for.

Try **Love Inspired® Romance Larger-Print** books and fall in love with inspirational romances that take you on an uplifting journey of faith, forgiveness and hope.

Try **Love Inspired® Suspense Larger-Print** books where courage and optimism unite in stories of faith and love in the face of danger.

Or TRY BOTH!

In return, we ask just one favor: Would you please participate in our brief Reader Survey? We'd love to hear from you.

This FREE BOOKS GIVEAWAY means that we pay for *everything!* We'll even cover the shipping, and no purchase is necessary, now or later. So please return your survey today. You'll get **Two Free Books** and **Two Mystery Gifts** from each series to try, altogether worth over **$20!**

Sincerely

Pam Powers

Pam Powers
For Harlequin Reader Service

Complete the survey below and return it today to receive up to **4 FREE BOOKS** and **FREE GIFTS** guaranteed!

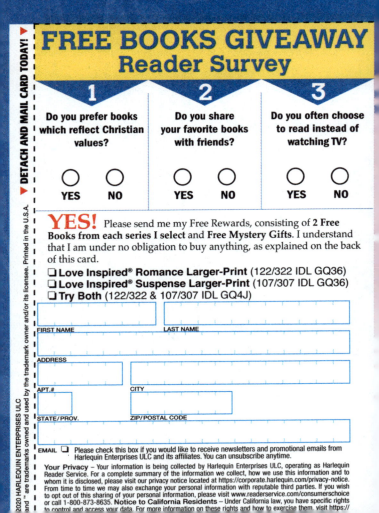

▼ DETACH AND MAIL CARD TODAY!

FREE BOOKS GIVEAWAY
Reader Survey

1
Do you prefer books which reflect Christian values?

○ YES ○ NO

2
Do you share your favorite books with friends?

○ YES ○ NO

3
Do you often choose to read instead of watching TV?

○ YES ○ NO

YES! Please send me my Free Rewards, consisting of **2 Free Books from each series I select** and **Free Mystery Gifts**. I understand that I am under no obligation to buy anything, as explained on the back of this card.

❏ **Love Inspired® Romance Larger-Print** (122/322 IDL GQ36)
❏ **Love Inspired® Suspense Larger-Print** (107/307 IDL GQ36)
❏ **Try Both** (122/322 & 107/307 IDL GQ4J)

FIRST NAME   LAST NAME

ADDRESS

APT.#   CITY

STATE/PROV.   ZIP/POSTAL CODE

EMAIL ❏ Please check this box if you would like to receive newsletters and promotional emails from Harlequin Enterprises ULC and its affiliates. You can unsubscribe anytime.

Your Privacy – Your information is being collected by Harlequin Enterprises ULC, operating as Harlequin Reader Service. For a complete summary of the information we collect, how we use this information and to whom it is disclosed, please visit our privacy notice located at https://corporate.harlequin.com/privacy-notice. From time to time we may also exchange your personal information with reputable third parties. If you wish to opt out of this sharing of your personal information, please visit www.readerservice.com/consumerschoice or call 1-800-873-8635. **Notice to California Residents** – Under California law, you have specific rights to control and access your data. For more information on these rights and how to exercise them, visit https://

▲ If offer card is missing write to: Harlequin Reader Service, P.O. Box 1341, Buffalo, NY 14240-8531 or visit www.ReaderService.com ▲

BUSINESS REPLY MAIL
FIRST-CLASS MAIL   PERMIT NO. 717   BUFFALO, NY

POSTAGE WILL BE PAID BY ADDRESSEE

HARLEQUIN READER SERVICE
PO BOX 1341
BUFFALO NY 14240-8571

NO POSTAGE
NECESSARY
IF MAILED
IN THE
UNITED STATES

"Most of you know Natalie, Aidan's mom." He introduced her to his sisters-in-law, Tori and Isabella.

Evan's stepmom, Claudia, stood. Her light brown wavy hair with fine strands of silver brushed her shoulders. She wore a light green T-shirt advertising the Fatigues to Farming program and white Bermuda shorts. She wrapped Natalie in an unexpected hug. "It's so nice to see you again, Natalie. Evan's been talking about you and Aidan constantly."

Natalie scanned the older woman's face, not finding even a hint of anger. "Nice to see you, too."

Evan's father, Chuck, pushed to his feet and made his way over to them. He placed a hand on Natalie's shoulder and gave it a gentle squeeze. He smiled. "Good to see you again, Natalie."

Wait. What?

Chuck crouched in front of Aidan. "Hey, Aidan. It's nice to meet you."

Aidan edged closer to Evan. "Are you really my grandpa?"

Chuck's eyes darted between Aidan and Natalie. He blinked rapidly and swallowed a couple of times before he answered. "I sure am." Then he jerked a thumb over his shoulder. "Landon and Livie call me Papa, but you can call me whatever you want."

Aidan stared at him a moment, then grinned, looking so much like Evan. "I have a grandpa. Now I have a papa, too. That's cool."

"Want to meet the twins?" Chuck pushed to his feet and held out his hand.

Releasing Evan's hand, Aidan took Chuck's as if it was the most natural thing to do.

As they passed her, Chuck cupped her shoulder again

and gave it another gentle squeeze. Despite the affectionate gesture, Natalie could see the hurt in his eyes.

If only she could go back to fix the past...

An hour later, conversation swirled around her as twilight dusted the horizon. Natalie sat in her chair taking in the lively family. Daisy lay at her feet watching the activity.

Jake's wife, Tori, who was also Claudia's niece, sat in a coral-colored chair with her caramel-colored hair twisted in a messy bun and looking utterly adorable in her fitted floral T-shirt that stretched over her baby bump. Her dog, Poppy, a black-and-tan Yorkie, lay on her lap.

With her dark brown hair in a braid that fell over the front of her right shoulder, Isabella, Tucker's fiancée, sat next to him with her eyes closed and a smile on her face as they entwined hands.

Being best friends with Willow for so many years, it was hard for Natalie to imagine Tucker married to anyone other than Willow's older sister, Rayne. But after Tucker had lost his first wife so tragically from an allergic reaction, Natalie was thrilled to see he had found a second chance at love.

Around her the conversation was relaxed and breezy.

Natalie needed to chill.

The moment she let her guard down, though, surely one of Evan's family members was going to ask the question she most dreaded—why did she keep Aidan away?

No one would understand, and she'd just make a mess of things like she had with Evan.

She longed to escape.

But with Aidan racing around the yard with his newfound cousins, she couldn't take him away just because she was uncomfortable.

"Mom, check out this huge bubble." Aidan ran toward her with his lime-green elongated wand stretched out in front of him, balancing a basketball-sized bubble on top.

"Whoa!" She reached for her phone and snapped a picture, which she texted to Evan.

Then Aidan swiveled toward Evan, who slouched in his chair next to her. As Aidan approached, he straightened and pulled his legs up so the boy wouldn't trip over his feet.

Once Aidan had made his rounds showing off his giant bubble to the rest of the family, he ran off after Landon and Olivia.

Each one of Evan's family members treated Aidan with the same care and compassion as they did Evan's twin niece and nephew.

Maybe she was worried for nothing.

Evan's brother Tucker cleared his throat, then leaned forward in his chair, keeping Isabella's hand tucked in his. "So after Bella agreed to marry me last month, we've been trying to pick a date."

Isabella curled her arm through his elbow. "Since we feel it's best for me to be moved in before the twins go back to school, we would like to get married at the end of the month. That gives us less than three weeks, but we just want a small wedding with family and close friends."

As the Holland clan peppered them with questions, Natalie longed to sprint to her car and head down the hill to her parents' place, where she could escape back to her comfort zone.

Evan drained the water out of his reusable bottle, then

stood and dropped the empty container in his chair. He moved behind her, settled his hands on her shoulders and lowered his head near her ear. "I need to stretch my legs. Wanna go for a walk?"

She nodded and searched the yard for her son. As if sensing the direction of her thoughts, Evan gave her shoulders a gentle squeeze. "He'll be fine. We won't be gone long." He looked over at his father. "Hey, Dad. We're going for a short walk. Mind keeping an eye on Aidan?"

"No problem." Chuck waved them away as he watched the kids race around the yard with their bubble wands and the dogs chasing them.

Reaching for Daisy's leash, Natalie stood and fell in step with Evan as they crossed the yard to the road.

Shades of rose-gold and violet crowned the hilltops as the sun lowered behind the trees. Clouds stretched like pulled cotton candy across the vast sky.

"Everything looks so big up here." Sliding Daisy's leash onto her wrist, Natalie buried her hands in the front pocket of her pullover hoodie.

Beside her, Evan released a deep sigh. "Yes, it does. Listen, Nat, I've been doing a lot of thinking since yesterday." He stopped, picked a white daisy growing along the fence line and held it out to her. "What do you think about us getting married? For Aidan's sake?"

Taking it, she stared at him. The python grip around her stomach uncoiled and snaked upward, squeezing her lungs.

No way she'd heard him correctly…

"Are you asking me to marry you?"

He reached for another flower and plucked each of the white petals until one remained. He rubbed his chin, then looked at her with a boyish grin toying at the corner of his mouth. "Yeah, I guess I am."

Natalie didn't know whether to laugh or cry. Still holding the flower, she folded her arms over her chest. "I love my…*our* son more than anything in the world. And I will do almost anything to ensure he has a good life. But I won't marry you."

"Why not?"

"Seriously? How can you even ask that?" Natalie grabbed his arm. "Evan William Holland, look me in the eye and tell me you love me. Tell me you're ready for us to spend the rest of our lives together. Tell me you want to marry me more than anything else in the world. Tell me you've forgiven me for keeping Aidan from you. Answer yes to all of those—and then I will marry you."

Evan's gaze shifted to over her shoulder. The flower drifted out his fingers, falling at her feet.

She dropped his arm, her throat thickening and her vision blurring. "That's what I thought. Our son is not a good enough reason to get married."

The look on his face nearly crushed her heart.

He reached over and brushed his thumb over her cheekbone. "I loved you, you know. I wanted to marry you, raise a family with you. I wanted to spend the rest of my life with you."

She cupped her hand over his. "Oh, Ev. You weren't ready. Between losing your mom, your family falling apart, Micah taking off and then Ben getting killed, your heart was too broken to consider settling down. The river was calling and you needed to answer."

"How do you know I'm not ready now?" He lifted his injured shoulder. "The river won't be calling anymore."

"I know because you're talking in the past tense.

River water flows in your veins and it always will. I never should have kept Aidan from you. I can't apologize enough for that. You can see him whenever you want, keep him whenever possible, but getting married is not the answer. If I do get married someday, it will be to someone who loves me and wants to be with me. Not just for the sake of my child. I will not risk that."

Puffing out his cheeks, Evan released a breath. He shoved his hands into his pockets and kicked at the dirt around the fence post. Evan nodded, then he eyed her and shrugged. "Okay, then. Marriage is out, so how about dinner? Just you and me."

"Evan…"

He held up his hand. "One dinner. What's the harm in that?"

The harm would come when she fell in love with him a second time. And got her heart broken after he realized she was more trouble than she was worth.

But her mother kept telling her to give him a chance.

And it was only dinner.

"All right," she answered quietly.

His head whipped up as a grin spread across his face. "Really?"

She nodded.

And hoped she didn't regret it.

Why had Evan allowed Nat to talk him into doing an escape room of all places?

After she'd shocked him by saying yes to dinner, he'd hoped they'd have a quiet meal getting to know each other all over again without the distractions of their families and animals. He'd wanted to follow that with a walk under the stars or something.

The last thing he'd expected was sharing a cramped table in the noisy Mexican restaurant with Willow and her date, Julian.

Evan loved Willow. When her older sister had been married to his brother Tucker, Evan and his brothers had kind of adopted her into the family, treating her like a little sister. She and Micah had been pretty tight. Then, after Rayne died so tragically, they'd made sure Willow had the support she needed.

Tonight, though, he wasn't in the mood to hang out with her and her date. After he'd picked up Nat, she'd asked if he minded a last-minute double date.

What could he say? Really.

So he ate his Texano burrito, smiled and laughed in the right places, and tried not to knock into Julian's tangle of legs under the table.

But now as he stood on the sidewalk outside the escape room place, a trickle of sweat slid down his spine. And it had nothing to do with the lingering fire in his chest from the jalapeño peppers he'd eaten or the eighty-five-degree sunshine beating down on them.

He tried to pay attention to the escape room host who met them at the door dressed as a butler. Evan should have listened to the directions. Instead, his eyes roamed over the caricature images of people stickered on the windows looking puzzled, scared or trapped.

Trapped.

He understood that feeling way too well.

Where was River when he needed him?

Feeling he wouldn't need his dog tonight, he'd left River at home with Toby in his father's care. Now he missed the grip of River's lead and the comforting nuzzle of his nose against his hand.

Natalie slid her hand into his elbow. She looked up at him and smiled sweetly. "Ready?"

No.

He nodded and tightened his hand into a fist.

She wore a white sundress patterned with yellow sunflowers, a short jean jacket to cover her shoulders and navy sandals. Her hair lay in loose waves around her shoulders. Every time she moved, it released a scent that made him want to comb his fingers through the silky curls.

They followed Willow and Julian into the main lobby, which reminded him of a movie theater minus the scent of popcorn. Crimson carpet muffled their steps as they faced four men wearing dark sunglasses and black suits, looking like secret service agents. Each one stood in front of a numbered door.

Their butler host ushered them to door three, where six strangers stood, waiting. "Welcome to Granny Maude's attic. You will have one hour to watch Granny's message, then search for clues to find her hidden will. If you find it before the timer runs out, you will be able to claim your inheritance. Any questions?"

Evan's eyes darted around the room. Where was the nearest exit?

Spy guy number three stepped away from the door as James the Butler unlocked the door and opened it with a flourish. "Good luck, and we'll see you on the other side."

Other side? Other side of what?

He swallowed. Hard. And trailed behind the others as they climbed creaky stairs. His muscles tightened as the door closed behind them and the lock turned, trapping them inside.

They entered a small, old-fashioned parlor with high-backed furniture, round tables with lacy cloths, and tall windows with heavy drapes. The air was musty and smelled faintly of floral perfume.

Julian rubbed his hands together. "Let's start looking for clues."

Willow placed a hand on his arm. "Wait. We need to listen to Granny's message."

She scanned the room, then stopped in front of an old-fashioned boxy television. She flicked on one of the knobs.

The screen rolled and flickered, and then an elderly woman appeared, her steel-gray hair pulled back in a tight bun. She wore a long-sleeved flowered dress, and glasses connected to a chain sat on her long, narrow nose.

She talked about her family trying to steal the fortune for themselves, so she'd hidden clues.

Then the screen went black.

One of the other participants looked at them. "I've done this before. If it opens, check it for clues. If you can take it off the wall, look for clues. We have fifty-five minutes left. Let's go."

The group scattered, leaving Evan standing by himself in the middle of the room. The pedestal clock on the fireplace ticked loudly. The sounds of doors slamming, frames being lifted off walls, and drawers being opened and closed crashed over him.

He needed to move, to help find clues, but his feet remained rooted to the floor.

Had those walls just moved?

Sweat beaded on his lip and slicked his skin. Pressure mounted in his chest. His heartbeat thundered in his ears. He tried to take a breath, but the stale, stuffy air clogged his throat.

He squeezed a palm over his eyes.

Get a grip, man.

His breathing shuddered as lights swirled behind his eyes.

He needed to get out of there.

Forcing his feet to move, he pounded down the steps and rammed a shoulder against the bottom door. One of the suited dudes jumped back as Evan rushed past.

He pushed through the exit door, gripped his knees and sucked in a lungful of air. Spying a bench outside the entrance, he sat and buried his face in his shaking hands.

Someone sat next to him.

He didn't need to open his eyes to know it was Natalie. The scent of her body lotion announced her arrival.

Talk about making a great impression on their date. Instead of showing her how good they could be together, he'd ended up making a fool of himself and embarrassing her.

She pressed a hand on his arm. "Hey, are you all right?"

He nodded, feeling the heat climb up his neck. "Wanna get out of here?"

She stood and stretched out a hand.

He looked at her long fingers, then lifted his eyes to her face. Without a word, he took her hand, stood and waited.

Was she going to let go?

Instead of giving her the option, he twined his fingers through hers, allowing the warmth of her touch to flow through him.

They walked hand in hand to his truck in silence. He

opened her door and helped her inside, then rounded the front to climb behind the wheel. After starting the engine, he blasted the AC to clear the stuffy cab. Natalie shrugged off her jean jacket.

Their silence continued as they drove back to Shelby Lake. He should probably take her home but didn't want to end their date on a sour note. Somehow, he needed to redeem himself, salvage the rest of the evening so she'd give him another chance.

He drove up Holland Hill, past the farm and turned onto his property next to his RV. He shut off the engine and shifted in his seat. "I'll be right back."

Inside his RV, he pulled out two bottles of water from the small fridge. Then he dragged his sleeping bag off his unmade bunk and made his way back outside.

Natalie stood by his truck with her arms wrapped around her waist. Evan rounded to the bed of the truck, released the tailgate and spread out the sleeping bag. He dropped the water on the blanket. Standing in front of her, he rested his hands at her waist and then lifted her onto the tailgate. He hopped up beside her.

Natalie crossed her ankles and stared up at the sky smudged with smoky clouds and burnished gold.

"Hey, Nat. Listen, I'm sorry if I embarrassed you."

She turned to him and frowned. "Embarrassed me? How?"

"By abandoning the escape room like a scared eight-year-old."

She pressed a hand to his shoulder. "Evan. I don't care about that. I'm sorry for even suggesting it."

"What about Willow and Julian?"

Nat lifted a shoulder. "I texted her to say you weren't

feeling well and we had to leave. It gives her more time alone with Julian anyway."

He reached over and gave her hand a gentle squeeze. "Thanks."

She looked at him with the barest hint of a smile on her face. "No problem. It's so peaceful out here."

In the distance, cows sounded from the barn while the crickets serenaded them. The wind stroked their faces. Water burbled in the creek while bullfrogs croaked.

"Yeah, it's pretty great. When I was a kid, I used to haul my sleeping bag out to the field when no one else was around. I'd lay on my back, fold my arms behind my neck, and stare up at the sky. It was so huge. The stars twinkled like tiny flashlights, and even though I was by myself, I never felt alone. I could breathe. Nothing was closing in on me even as darkness fell. I miss that."

"You miss what?" Nat's voice came out as a whisper, almost as if she was afraid to disturb the solitude.

"I miss being able to breathe."

"Like in the escape room?"

He nodded.

"You told Aidan about getting trapped in the hay. That must have been traumatic for you. How often do you struggle with claustrophobia?"

He gripped the edge of the tailgate and shrugged. "I don't know. I just…" He sighed. "Do you remember what I said when I told Aidan about the hay fort I'd made?"

She nodded.

"What I didn't tell him was what happened when the fort collapsed."

"What did you do?"

"I yelled for my brothers, but none of them came. The hay dust caused my asthma to flare up. I started coughing and struggled to catch my breath. I was pretty scared."

"Sounds like it."

"I made it out, no thanks to my brothers, who ditched me."

"They ditched you?"

"They got tired of looking for me, so they headed into the house to watch some stupid cartoon."

"How'd that make you feel?"

"You playing shrink all of a sudden?"

She nudged his shoulder. "Knock it off."

He shrugged. "I felt…like I wasn't worth their time to be found. It taught me I could only depend on myself. And not to be put in situations where I'd feel trapped."

"Like your kayaking accident?"

He nodded. "That one still messes with my head. I really miss hanging out with my team, being on the water, but the truth is, the thought of stepping foot in a kayak again sends my heart slamming against my ribs. I know once I do it again, I'll be fine." He gave her a wry grin. "The place where I feel the most at home is creating the most fear in me right now. Ridiculous, huh?"

"It's understandable."

"When life gets overwhelming, I just want to slow down and take a deep breath. Lately, it's been a struggle to catch my breath. I screwed up, and now I feel like the biggest disappointment."

"Evan, you're such an amazing, stand-up guy. The disappointment you're feeling is all one-sided. If only you could see yourself the way others do."

Evan jerked his head toward her. Did she realize what she'd said? Who she was talking to?

She took his hand and turned it to trace the tattoo of

a sturdy oak tree on his left forearm. "I remember when you got this."

"Jake, Tuck, Micah and I got this same tattoo after Mom was killed. There's a tree near the farmhouse that remained unchanged even though the tornado nearly wiped out everything else. Dad had said our family was like that tree—Holland strong and rooted deep to weather any storm."

"And you will get through this, too."

"I'm just not sure what my future holds now." He curled his fingers around hers. "You're a great listener. You always have been. What about you? What do you want?"

"At least you can look to your future."

He frowned. "What do you mean by that?"

Natalie shifted her eyes toward the open field where wildflowers swayed in the breeze, cows called from a distance and the wind toyed with her hair. Sadness shadowed her eyes despite the smile curving her lips. "Peace. I long for peace."

"Like world peace?"

Nat shook her head and tapped her fist against her chest. "Peace in here. Peace to stop running."

Evan closed his fingers over hers. "What are you running from?"

Her eyes glazed with wetness and shimmered in the moonlight. "If I tell you, I will lose everything."

Before he could ask what she meant by that, she leaned over and brushed her lips across his, silencing him.

He cupped her face in his hands and deepened the kiss.

Chapter Nine

It was just a kiss. And not even her first kiss. Or even the first with Evan.

But it was her first one since she'd ended their relationship over five years ago.

Being wrapped in his arms again felt so right...and so wrong at the same time.

She shouldn't allow herself to get close to him. But when he looked at her with those blue eyes swimming in vulnerability, she shut off her brain and listened to her heart.

Needing to put some distance between them, Natalie loosened her arms around him and pressed her forehead against his.

She slipped out of Evan's arms, slid off the tailgate and then wrapped her arms around her waist. With her legs still feeling like jelly, she stared at the diamond-studded sky that shrouded them in darkness.

The metal creaked as Evan jumped off the bed of the truck, landing with a thud on the ground. A moment later, one of the truck doors opened, then closed again.

He moved behind Natalie, the hairs on the back of

her neck detecting his presence. He wrapped something soft around her shoulders. She detected the scent of his soap and realized it was a zip-up hoodie.

She slid her arms in the sleeves and zipped the jacket halfway, resisting the urge to bury her nose in the fabric. She smiled up at him. "Thanks."

He wrapped an arm around her waist and brushed the backs of his knuckles across her cheekbone. "I should take you home. Or find another way to keep you warm."

He lowered his head, but she pressed a hand against his chest. "Evan, we can't."

"Can't what? I'm simply holding you." He flashed her a boyish grin that reminded her of their son.

"And you were about to kiss me."

He reached for her hand. "Are you complaining?"

"You know it's not a good idea." She tried to step out of his embrace.

He drew her close again. "Actually, I think it's a pretty good idea. You must have thought so, too, because you were the one who kissed me."

"Yeah, but I did that because…"

"Because why? You find me charming? Totally irresistible?"

Her cheeks warmed and she turned away. "I kissed you because…" She sighed. "I kissed you because I didn't want to answer your question."

Evan loosened his hold and frowned at her. "What question?"

"You mentioned you weren't sure what your future holds. I said at least you could look to the future."

"Right. I asked what you meant, and you kissed me." That grin slid in place once again, which caused her heart to shift.

Her cheeks warmed. "Yeah."

"So, what did you mean?" His gentle tone, low and throaty, invited her to open up to him.

And she wanted to. But…

She pressed a hand to his chest again. "Evan, there are some things in my past that may change how you feel about me." She closed her eyes against the mounting pressure, then opened them to find him looking at her with such compassionate concern. "I want to tell you but, honestly, I just don't want to get into it tonight. Can we table this conversation for another time with the promise that I will share with you?"

He ran the tips of his fingers over her cheek and then pressed a kiss against her forehead. He gathered her into the security of his arms and rested his chin on top of her head. "Sweet Nat, I won't pressure you to share anything you don't want to tell me. Just know I'm always here for you, ready to listen."

Hearing those words lifted some of the burdens off her heart. She glanced at her watch. "It's getting late."

He nodded and tipped up her chin. "I'll be here when you're ready to talk. Maybe I can help."

She shook her head, blinking back another rush of tears, and turned away from him. Despite the too-big hoodie, she shivered and rubbed her hands over her arms. Then she faced him again. "Thank you, Evan, but you can't. No one can. This is my cross to bear. Would you mind taking me home?"

"Of course not." Evan moved to the passenger side of the truck, opened the door and helped her in. He rounded the front, climbed behind the wheel and started the engine. They headed down the hill in silence.

A few minutes later, Evan pulled into the Bishops'

driveway and left the engine running. He draped an arm over the steering wheel and looked at her. "Will you go to church with me tomorrow?"

She jerked her gaze up. "Church? I didn't realize you attended."

"I do when I can. Now that I'm home, I attend with the family."

She released the seat belt, removed his hoodie, already missing the warmth it offered, and grabbed her jean jacket. "No, thanks. I don't do church."

"Why not?"

"There's no point. God picks and chooses whose prayers He answers—I wasn't chosen, so I stopped praying. Why bother going to church?"

"You know, Nat, I've had similar thoughts, but a wise man once told me, 'God won't ever give up on you. If anyone walks away, it will be you.'"

"Who told you that?"

"Your dad. And he was right. I haven't always made the best choices, but despite my screwups, God's still there for me."

"I appreciate your faith, but I was an innocent child who cried into her pillow night after night, begging God to listen to my prayers. He stayed silent."

Evan cupped her cheek and brushed his thumb over her skin. "I don't know what you've gone through, but I hope you can trust me enough someday to share. Just know I'm here for you."

Natalie pulled his hand away and simply held it. "Why are you so kind to me, Evan? What I did was horrible. What did you say—unforgivable?"

"I reacted out of anger. I know you have your reasons. Someday, you'll tell me, and then we can move forward." Releasing her hand, he opened his door and stepped down. Then he came around to her side and helped her out.

Always the gentleman.

They walked to the door, where the porch light shone overhead like it had when Natalie was in high school and out with friends.

The glow of the amber light highlighted the sculpted planes of Evan's face.

He trailed a knuckle over her cheekbone. She wanted to turn her face toward the warmth of his touch, but she didn't move, afraid to break the moment.

"Nat, I'm always here for you. Anytime you want to talk. About anything." He leaned forward and kissed her forehead, barely brushing his lips over her skin. Without another word, he turned and stepped out of the circle of light and disappeared into the darkness.

A moment later, he backed out of the drive and disappeared down the road.

She was a fool, and she didn't deserve someone like Evan.

She pressed her back against the column and rested a hip on the front porch railing, replaying Evan's words over in her head.

What if she *did* take a chance? What if she unburdened her heart? Would Evan be able to handle the truth? Or maybe the lies, depending on his perspective. When he'd learned about Aidan, he'd said he couldn't forgive her. What if he learned the truth about who her biological father was and wanted nothing to do with her? Or worse yet—what if he used that truth to try to take Aidan from her?

For years, she had trusted only her parents and Ben.

After her brother was killed, her circle of trust had grown smaller.

What if she widened it by sharing her secrets with Evan?

She'd kept the past locked up for so long because the shadows that crept through her dreams filled her with anxiety, silencing her.

Trusting Evan meant risking everything she'd worked so hard to rebuild.

But it was time to put the past to rest and move forward.

She just hoped it didn't cost her more than what she could give.

Evan should've been walking on air.

After all, he somehow managed to redeem himself after the escape room meltdown.

And he kissed Nat.

Yeah, that was the highlight of the evening.

So why did he feel so weighed down?

Evan hoofed it down the quiet road. The sun, barely stretched across the horizon, cast an amber glow across the cornfields.

As he cut through the barnyard, chickens waddled in front of him and cows called through the open doorway of the barn. The morning dew wet his flip-flopped feet as he crossed the yard and took the back deck steps two at a time. He kicked off his shoes—Mom's long-ingrained rule still in his head even after her death—and scuffed his damp feet on the burly welcome mat.

The scent of fresh coffee and cooked bacon flavored the air, causing his stomach to grumble.

He opened the door and was greeted by Toby and

River, wagging their tails. Entering the kitchen, he rubbed their heads. "Hey, boys. Did you behave last night?"

"They sacked out on the living room rug and didn't move until I got up this morning." Dad sat at the kitchen table, his open Bible in front of him and a steaming cup of black coffee at his right hand.

The open Bible was as much a mainstay on the table as the salt and pepper shakers. Some of Evan's favorite memories had been waking up as a kid, heading into the kitchen for a bowl of cereal and finding his dad bent over his Bible, hands folded in prayer. Knowing he was included in those prayers gave Evan the courage to chase after his dreams.

And to return home when those dreams were destroyed.

"Morning, Dad. Thanks for keeping them." Evan placed a hand on his dad's shoulder and gave it a quick squeeze before moving to the counter. He pulled a mug out of the cupboard and filled it with coffee.

Dad looked up from reading, slurped his coffee and held his cup out for Evan to top it off. "Morning. You stay at your RV last night?"

Leaning against the sink, Evan took a sip, allowing the rich goodness to slide down his throat, and nodded. "I got back late and didn't want disturb you and Claudia. Wouldn't mind using the shower, though."

Dad waved a hand toward the ceiling. "Have at it. You know where everything is. How'd last night go?"

"It was…" Evan didn't want to tell his father about his freak-out at the escape room, but he'd understand. "It wasn't the best date. When I picked Nat up, she asked if I'd mind doubling with Willow and her date. We had

Mexican food, then ended up at an escape room with half a dozen strangers."

"An escape room? Huh."

"Yeah. I managed about ten minutes before the walls started closing in. So I humiliated myself by rushing out of the building and nearly passing out on the sidewalk. Natalie came after me. We left and went to my place."

His father lifted an eyebrow.

Evan held up a hand. "Relax. We sat on my tailgate and talked about my claustrophobia. I told her about the hay fort caving in."

"You tell her about your recent accident?"

He nodded. "A little. And I mentioned about not knowing what the future holds. Something bad happened to her, but she didn't want to get into it. I'm hoping she'll open up soon. You know anything about it?"

Dad rubbed a callused hand over his chin and toyed with his spoon. "That's something you're gonna have to hear from Natalie."

"So you do know."

"Not my story to tell. Give her time and she may come around. She needs to learn how to trust people."

"I invited her to church. She said God picked and chose which prayers He answered, so she didn't see the point."

"How'd that make you feel?"

"Conflicted."

"About what?"

Evan dragged a hand through his hair. "While we're racing through the competition circuit, my church attendance is sporadic, but the River Rats…well, we did our own Sunday morning get-togethers. One of my teammates, Preach, would read scripture and we'd talk about it, then have a time of prayer. His wife, Tasha, played songs on her ukulele. It may not have been a white building with a steeple, but God was there."

"Church isn't a building or place. It's a gathering of believers. The Bible tells us, 'where two or three are gathered together in My name, there am I in the midst of them.'"

Evan drained his cup, rinsed it and placed it inside the dishwasher. "I miss my team. They've been texting, asking when I'm heading back."

"I'm sure. They were a huge part of your life for the last five or so years. What'd you tell them?"

"I said I didn't know. PT's not going as well as I had hoped. And that I had some family business to tend to."

"Like Aidan?"

Evan nodded. "I didn't go into detail. I'm not embarrassed by him. I'm just not ready to share him with the team yet. I guess I'm being a little selfish and wanting to keep him to myself a bit longer."

"He seemed to have a good time with everyone the other night."

"Nat said he's been talking nonstop about Livie and Landon." Evan moved to the table and pulled out a chair. "Preach and Tasha remind me of you and Claudia."

"How so?"

"They lost their spouses, then found love again with each other. They didn't allow those tragedies to derail their faith."

"Unexpected love is a beautiful thing. Even when you think your heart isn't ready, God works within to make changes."

"I hope Nat will let Him make changes in her heart.

Otherwise, how can I let myself fall in love with her again if she's not willing to give God a chance?"

"You need to give it up to God and make a choice."

"Even if that choice means not being a family for our son?"

Dad moved out of his chair and rounded the table to stand in front of him, coffee cup in hand. "Evan, being in a spiritually mismatched relationship is challenging and could create more issues down the road. You and Natalie can be great co-parents even if your relationship keeps you only as friends. You're both an important part of his life. No matter what choices the two of you make, you're always going to be in each other's lives. But if you two don't agree on God, then you need to decide how you're going to proceed with that relationship. I'd hate to see you get your heart broken, and even more than that, I'd hate to see you change your relationship with the Lord to please a girl, no matter how pretty or important she may be."

"So you're saying I shouldn't pursue a relationship with Nat?"

"I'm saying give it up to God. And do what He directs. He's working in your life and in Natalie's, even if she doesn't see it." His father drained his cup, then set it upside down on the top rack of the dishwasher.

"Nat feels if I go back to paddling, I'm choosing my career over my son. She doesn't understand I can have both without walking away from him. Or her."

"That's her fear talking. Give her time." His dad glanced at the clock above the sink. "I'd better head upstairs and get ready for church so Claudia doesn't leave without me."

"Like that'll happen."

"Love you, son, And I promise you, God's got this. Let Him work it out."

"Love you, too, Dad. And thanks."

"Anytime." His father left the kitchen.

Evan snatched a piece of bacon off the paper-towel-covered plate on the stove, then looked out the kitchen window over the sink, soaking in his father's words,

Yes, he believed God was in control, but what if He didn't change Natalie's heart?

Then what? She was the only woman he'd ever loved. Being around her again roused those feelings he had buried for his heart's protection.

Maybe it would be best to put a little distance between them before someone got hurt.

Something was going on with Evan, and Natalie couldn't quite put her finger on it.

While he was perfectly nice and well-mannered, he seemed...a bit cool toward her.

She'd texted to see if he'd like to come over after church to pick blackberries, then stay for dinner. From the moment he arrived with Toby and River, he'd kept his distance. Well, mostly from her.

For the past half hour, he'd been playing catch with Aidan, throwing the white plastic ball and showing Aidan how to hit correctly with the yellow bat he brought for him. Not to mention the matching Holland Farms baseball hats.

Of course she wouldn't begrudge him his time with their son. But when he'd arrived, she wouldn't have minded more than a quick "Hey, Nat."

After their date last night, she thought they were moving closer together. Maybe she'd read more into it than what he'd intended.

What if he was tired of her keeping him at arm's length?

"He's good with Aidan."

A shadow fell over her as she stretched out on the chaise lounge. Caught up in her own thoughts, she hadn't heard the sliding glass doors to the patio open. She shaded her eyes and looked up to see her father next to her, holding two glasses of lemonade.

He handed one to her and set the other on the rectangular metal-and-stone-tile patio table. He pulled out a chair cushioned with the same hibiscus flower print as her chaise and sat with his hands folded behind his head. "Missy Chapman called. They're coming after dinner to pick up Miko. Mind helping me to get her ready?"

"Not at all. I bathed her while you and Mom were at church. Her things are gathered and waiting in her basket inside her suite. Once I feed her, we'll go for another walk, then she'll be ready to go."

"Thanks, Punky. I'm not sure how we would have managed if you hadn't come home to help out."

"Dad, that's what families do—they help each other."

"You uprooted your life, left your home and put your business on hold to be here for us. We really appreciate it."

"I know, and honestly, it wasn't that much of a sacrifice. By coming home, I'm still able to do what I love, and surround Aidan with family."

"You didn't have to leave, you know...after you learned you were pregnant. We would've helped you."

"I needed to learn how to be on my own."

"And what did you learn?"

"I hated it." Her vision blurred, remembering the loneliness that had blanketed way too often, when the wounds of her breakup had lingered, pricking her aching heart.

"Maybe my heart attack was an answer to a prayer in many ways. Of course, I don't want to be sick or add more stress on your mother, but it brought you back home and it forced me to slow down. Something your mother's been getting on me to do for years."

"Maybe."

"You disagree?"

"I don't spend a lot of time praying these days."

"Why not?"

"What's the point? God's selective in what prayers He answers. Mine never seemed to make the list, so I stopped asking. I remember being in that courtroom with the family services worker begging God to save our family, and He ignored me."

"Why do you feel He ignored you?"

"We went through some really hard times. God could have prevented that."

"You're right, but those difficulties strengthen your character."

"I was eight, Dad. Ben was ten. What did we know about character?"

"Maybe it was to bring your mother to a place where she needed to ask for help from your grandparents. Once you moved back to Shelby Lake, you were safe. You were surrounded by people who loved you and cared for you. No one was going to hurt you again. Even though your prayers weren't answered the minute you said them, that doesn't mean God wasn't working on your behalf."

Her father's words lingered in her thoughts as she

continued watching Evan and Aidan and snapping pictures with her phone.

Natalie swung her legs over the side of the chaise and stood. After draining her glass, she dropped a kiss on the top of Dad's head. "Thanks. I appreciate what you said. I need to see if those two still want to pick some berries before dinner."

Fifteen minutes later, blackberry stains on Aidan's mouth showed he had eaten more than he picked.

With her mother's fear of snakes, Dad kept the grass cut short between the rows of blackberry bushes that had been growing behind the house for as long as Natalie could remember. Berries ranging in color from pale pink to deep purple grew from their sturdy stems. Trying to avoid the prickers, she picked the plump purple berries and left the lighter ones to ripen.

"Dad, check out this big one." Aidan held a thumb-sized berry in his small palm.

Evan dropped a handful of berries in his bucket and checked out Aidan's trophy berry. "That's almost big enough for its own pie."

Natalie moved down the hedge behind her parents' house and peeked into Evan's bucket. It was nearly half full. "How do you pick so many so fast?"

He waved his berry-stained hands at her. "I use two hands. When we were kids, we went berry picking with Dad. We'd have a contest to see who could pick the most berries. Jake and Tuck always beat Micah and me."

"Well, there's no competition here. You have nothing to prove to me."

"Sure, I do. I have to prove I'm a good enough father. I have to prove that I'm not going to walk away. I'm proving my worth to you on a daily basis." Even though the baseball hat shadowed his face and he spoke with a smile in place, his words held an edge that didn't sit well with her.

Was that the impression she was giving off? Even after last night?

How could she let Evan know he had nothing to prove to her?

Chapter Ten

The last thing Natalie wanted to do was offend a client, especially one who had been a loyal customer for the last ten years. Despite the frozen smile on her face and the automatic nodding of her head, she was freaking out.

Of course, Evan was there when Missy Chapman, the wife of the owner of the local news station, arrived to pick up the dog they'd been boarding for the past week.

When Missy suggested showcasing the service dog training program as one of their news channel's human interest pieces, Evan jumped on the idea. Once he'd started talking about the service dog project partnered with his family's Fatigues to Farming program, there was no stopping him.

"So what do you think, Natalie? Would you like to be a part of this special feature?"

Natalie's heartbeat thundered in her ears, drowning out the tall redhead's words. She took a step back as her eyes darted around the yard searching for a place to escape. Maybe to hide.

Her body thrummed as a rush of adrenaline coursed through her.

She pulled in a shaky breath.

Somehow she needed to keep it together.

In just a few more minutes, Missy would head out. Then Natalie could talk Evan out of pursuing the dumb idea the woman had put in his head.

Except it wasn't a dumb idea.

It was a brilliant one. The publicity would benefit the Hollands' program.

However, Natalie wanted no part of it. She needed to figure out how to get out of it.

Once Missy backed her SUV out of the small lot and disappeared around the bend, Natalie sagged in the doorway.

Evan moved beside her. "Hey, you okay?"

She reached for the bin that held Missy's dog's belongings. "Not really."

"What's going on? I figured you'd be thrilled about this free publicity."

"Don't get me wrong—it's great. I…just don't want to be a part of it."

"Why not? Mrs. Chapman said they love human interest stories like this one and she could get great coverage for the service dog project, for the veterans, to raise awareness. Opportunities like that don't come along very often."

"I know. You should take it. Talk to your dad and your brothers. You guys will do a great job. Just count me out."

"But, Nat, you're an important part of this program—without Bishop Boarding & Kennels, I wouldn't have even gotten involved."

Natalie grabbed his arm. "Evan, if you decide to do

this, please promise me you will keep my family out of this. Me, Mom, Dad and definitely Aidan."

He rubbed a hand over a jaw, something she'd seen his father do so many times over the years. "I don't get it, Nat. What's going on? You think it's a great opportunity, yet you don't want anything to do with it?"

She coiled Daisy's leash around her hand, focusing on keeping the lines straight and smooth. "I don't want to be on camera."

"I know you're shy, but I've seen the way you've handled clients. You're warm and generous, and once you start talking about the program, you light up and everything else seems to disappear."

"That's not what I mean."

"Then what? Help me to understand."

She shook her head. "I can't."

"Why not?"

"Because…"

"Great answer."

She scoffed and shook her head again. Why did Evan even put up with her? She was being ridiculous, but she didn't know what else she could say to protect the secret buried deep within her.

She'd known Evan for a large chunk of her life, and, yes, her secret would be safe with him.

By sharing it, she risked exposing…and losing everything she loved.

The rational side of her thinking reminded her how implausible that fear was of actually coming true. But then her anxiety kicked into overdrive, drowning out common sense.

She lifted her face to find Evan watching her. His blue

eyes filled with kindness and compassion. His strong hands were inches from hers.

Evan, strong and loyal, who put others before himself. Evan, who chased big dreams. Evan, who was proving to be a fantastic father. Evan, who had stolen her heart years ago.

She couldn't deny it anymore.

She was falling in love with him all over again.

And if she loved him, then he deserved to know the truth.

Unwinding the dog's leash off her hand, she flexed her fingers and held out a hand to Evan. "Let's go for a walk."

He glanced back at the yard. "What about Aidan?"

"He's busy helping Dad feed the dogs. I'll let them know where we're going."

After informing her dad, she returned to the yard, still feeling her father's kiss on her forehead. She nodded toward the road. "Let's go."

With Daisy and Toby at their sides, they headed down the quiet, tree-lined country road that led to the new trail to Evan's property across the creek.

"I've always loved living here. We're only a couple of minutes from town, but we're still secluded enough to enjoy the peace and quiet."

"That's important to you, isn't it?"

Nat nodded.

"Other than when I'm chasing rivers, I've lived here all my life—born and raised on the hill."

"You're fortunate to have such a wonderful family, Evan. I hope you never take that for granted."

"Losing Mom gutted me. I've learned the value of gratitude. You can lose everything in a short minute."

Oh, how she knew…

She stopped and tightened her grip on the leash. She looked at Evan, then shifted her gaze to over his shoulder where the tree branches dipped and swayed with the gentle breeze stirring the leaves. "I need to tell you something, but you have to promise not to breathe a word of this to anyone—not your dad, your brothers, anyone. Promise me."

Evan frowned, concern wrinkling his forehead. "What's going on, Nat?"

"Promise me, Evan."

"Yes, I promise."

With her heart hammering against her ribs and feeling suddenly chilled by the warm breeze, Natalie dragged a shaky hand through her hair. She dug in her front pockets looking for a hair tie, but they were empty.

A feeling she knew too well.

Wrapping her arms around herself, she lifted her eyes to Evan and blew out a breath. "My name…my name is not Natalie Bishop."

"Wha—"

She held out a hand. She had to get this out. Because any moment now she was about to turn and race back to the house, run up to her room and lock the door.

But she wasn't a child anymore. She was a grown woman who needed to face her past.

"I was born Jessica Ann Henderson. Ted is not my biological father."

Evan's eyes widened, but he didn't say anything. Which she appreciated.

"Honestly, Ev, my past sounds more like a cable movie." She let out a strangled laugh. Tears pressed against the backs of her eyes. "My real father—Brady

Henderson—had a gambling addiction. He left all the time, promising he'd be back. We never knew when he'd return or what kind of mood he'd be in. I learned he couldn't be counted on. When I was eight, I woke up in the middle of the night to my parents fighting. Apparently, my father had gambled away the rent money, and we were being evicted. My father promised to come up with the money to prevent that from happening. He left and didn't come back."

"Nat, I'm sorry. No wonder you felt like I had abandoned you."

She lifted a shoulder. He was right, but she needed to get out the rest of the story before detouring down a rabbit hole.

"Mom worked two part-time jobs, but it wasn't enough. For a week, we slept in our car—the one thing my father managed not to gamble away. We'd go to a fast-food place for breakfast, and Mom would wash us up in the bathroom before taking us to school. She tried to call it a great adventure, but even at eight years old, I knew something wasn't right. Apparently, before we were evicted, my father stole money from his job to feed his addiction and ended up getting fired. One day at school, I told my best friend about our so-called great adventure, but I didn't realize my teacher could hear us. She ended up calling child protective services. All because I couldn't keep a secret."

"Nat, you were a child—it wasn't your fault. You were a victim of your circumstances."

"Regardless, Ben and I were placed in temporary foster care and went through the court system."

A fragment of a memory floated through her thoughts. Screaming for her mother over and over as a social worker carried her writhing body out of the cold, gray courtroom.

She forced herself back to the present. "While that was happening, my father robbed a convenience store and ended up being chased by police. I can't remember where he holed up, but somehow, he managed to call my mom at work for help. Instead of helping, she turned him in, and he was arrested. He blamed her and vowed to find her and make her pay. The media coverage was unbelievable. My grandparents came and rescued us. We ended up moving to New York to live with them, leaving behind everything I had known and starting over. That included new names."

"Why new names?"

"To protect us from my father's messes. It became national news because my father's crimes crossed state lines and the FBI had to get involved. Mom divorced my father, then his parental rights were terminated on grounds of abandonment. She created new identities, a new life, a fresh start for us."

"I'm sorry for all that you have gone through."

Natalie lifted a shoulder. "We're better off. She met Ted Bishop, who treated Ben and me like his own. After he and Mom got married, he asked if he could adopt us and be a part of his family. The day our adoption was finalized, Dad gave me a puppy named Shiloh, which means peace. She had been abandoned by her family. Soon after Mom and Ted married, we moved to Shelby Lake when he was offered the coaching job. Once Mom opened her clinic, Dad opened the kennels. The dogs were therapeutic. From that moment on, I knew I wanted to use animals to bring comfort to others."

"You're an amazing woman, Natalie, especially for

everything you've been through." Evan wrapped her in his arms and drew her against him. "Thank you for trusting me enough to share that with me. Is it safe to assume you don't want the media coverage because of the memories it brings up?"

"Maybe. Partly. Even though I know it's not rational—and Mom keeps telling me it's not going to happen—I have this fear that Brady will see the coverage and find us."

When Evan opened his mouth to speak, Natalie held up a hand. "I know it's not going to happen, but like I said, it's an irrational fear. That's another reason I kept Aidan from you—you were doing well in your career. I saw an interview Dad was watching, and I didn't want Aidan caught up in that publicity. Also, if someone started digging, they could uncover our past. Mom's worked so hard to put that behind her. Discovering where we came from could destroy everything all over again."

"Nat, I can't even imagine the trauma you've endured. But you're not alone in this. I'll do whatever I can to keep you and Aidan safe, do whatever it takes to put those fears to rest."

She searched his face. No traces of anger lingered in his eyes about her betrayal of who she really was. "You're not mad?"

"Mad? About what?"

"I—I lied to you…about who I was, where I came from. I'm the daughter of a liar, a thief."

He tipped up her chin and brushed the barest of kisses across her lips. "You didn't do it to be deceitful, but to protect yourselves. Coach adopted you and gave you a new name, a new identity, a fresh start. You can't change where you've come from, but you can change where you're going. I will help you as much I can."

The sincerity in his eyes was nearly her undoing. She pressed her ear against his chest and listened to the steady drumming of his heart. She closed her eyes and breathed in the scent of sunshine and fabric softener from his T-shirt.

Being in Evan's arms felt so good and so right. Life had been a difficult teacher, proving nothing lasted forever. But, oh, how she wanted to lean into Evan's words and believe them to be true.

What if she did all of that and still ended up with a broken heart? Then what? She wouldn't have anywhere else to turn.

Was she willing to risk it?

Chapter Eleven

The last thing he wanted to do was to scare his son, but somehow Evan needed to get Aidan to trust him, to understand he was there to help and to protect him.

But he got it.

He did.

He remembered having similar fears when he was his son's age. The way that fear bubbled up and wrapped around him.

When Tucker and Isabella invited Aidan to go swimming with them, Nat had reservations until Evan suggested they go, too. Not that he wanted to invite himself... but like Aidan, his mother needed to trust.

Spending the afternoon at the lake had seemed like a great idea until he suggested it to Nat and Aidan. How could the son of a state swimming champion and grandson of an award-winning swim coach hate the water?

He glanced at the beach where Natalie had spread out a striped quilt. Daisy was curled up under a pop-up shade canopy on the blanket while Nat and Isabella sat in the sand helping Livie make a sandcastle. Landon romped in the water with Tucker.

With Nat's hair piled on top in a messy bun and her wearing a pink-and-white polka-dot cover-up over her matching one-piece swimsuit, Evan struggled to keep his attention on his son.

Clusters of pines, oaks and maples guarded the perimeter of the denim-blue lake. Across the water, a couple of paddlers launched orange and blue kayaks into the water.

Evan turned away and swallowed the sigh building his chest. Midafternoon sun beat down on his back as he stood in the waist-deep water with River and Toby paddling beside him. "Come on, Aidan. The water's great, and I won't let go of you, I promise."

With the afternoon breeze whisking the water off his bare skin, Evan moved to the edge of the dock and rested an arm on the gray, weather-beaten wood. He reached out to touch the little boy sitting on the middle of the dock with his knees pulled to his chest and his thin arms wrapped around his skinny legs. Aidan buried his face in his knees and shook his head from side to side.

Evan pulled himself out of the water, wincing at the strain on his shoulder. Man, he was getting soft without the daily paddling.

River and Toby jumped onto the dock beside him, shook their coats free of water, then sprawled on the sun-warmed wood.

He tucked a finger under Aidan's chin and lifted his face so Evan could see his eyes. "When I was your age, I was afraid of the water, too."

Aidan eyed him. "You were?"

Evan nodded. "My mom took us to the pool, and it looked so big. Kids were running everywhere, and for a little skinny kid, it was overwhelming. I was too afraid to try."

"What happened?"

"Mom signed me up for swim lessons with this very nice man named Ted Bishop."

"Hey, that's my grandpa's name."

"It sure is. Coach taught me how to swim. Now I love the water. If I get in over my head, I know how to handle myself."

A sudden image of being trapped under his kayak surfaced in his head. His skin grew cold, and a familiar pressure mounted in his chest. Closing his eyes a moment, he breathed in a lungful of air.

He was safe.

He blew out the air through his nose.

He was free.

River rested his head on Evan's thigh, warming his skin. Evan placed his hand on the dog's neck and soaked in his calming presence.

"I'm not strong and brave like you."

His son's tiny voice sent a surge of warmth through Evan's chest at the same moment it pinched his heart.

"Remember what I said before—strength and bravery come from within. You think superheroes are born brave?"

Aidan shrugged.

"Nope. They learned how to overcome difficult circumstances. Their bravery comes from here—" Evan tapped Aidan's head "—not here." He tapped his son's small biceps. "Believe in yourself, and you can do anything."

Evan caught a movement out of the corner of his eye. He turned to see a couple walking their dog. Spying them, the dog barked and tugged on its leash.

Beside him, River's ears perked, but he didn't move

his head off Evan's leg. Toby stilled, his ears on alert. "Toby, stay."

The dog remained where he was. "Good boy." Evan patted his neck and turned back to Aidan. "So, want to get your brave on? I won't let go. I'll keep you safe."

Aidan relaxed his hold on his knees. "You promise?"

Evan put his hand to his chest. "I promise."

Standing, Evan extended a hand to Aidan. "I promise not to let go, so now it's up to you to trust me."

"What's trust mean?"

"It means you believe my words are true."

Aidan looked at him a moment, then gazed at the lake. He scrambled to his feet the same time a loud woof echoed across the water.

Evan turned to shield Aidan. But instead of protecting his son, the turn of his hip grazed the child's side. Before Aidan could catch his balance, he landed in the water with a loud splash. "Dad!"

Heart thundering in his ears, Evan jumped into the lake and reached for Aidan. But he disappeared under the water.

"Aidan!"

Evan dived at him, caught the kid around the waist and hauled him to his chest.

Coughing and sputtering and crying, Aidan clung to Evan's left arm. Heat seared the joint but Evan tried to ignore it. "Hey, I'm right here."

"You pushed me!"

"I'm sorry, buddy. It was an accident."

"You broke your promise."

The four words were coughed out between chattering teeth, and his son's righteous anger clawed at Evan. Yes, technically, he did, but it wasn't done purposely, something his son wouldn't understand. At that moment, Aidan saw his own suffering and the feeling of being let down.

Oh, how Evan understood that.

Wasn't that how he'd been feeling toward God?

Evan wrapped his arms around his son. "I'm right here."

"I was scared." Aidan fisted a hand and slugged Evan in the chest. "I couldn't see you. I thought you were gone."

"I know, but I was there the whole time. I will never leave you." As the sound of his own words washed over him, a lump formed in Evan's throat.

"Aidan!" Natalie sprinted down the dock, her bare feet thundering against the wood. Reaching them, she knelt on the edge of the dock and flung an arm out to them. "Give him to me."

Evan tightened his left arm around Aidan, who had his arms wrapped around Evan's neck, and paddled to the dock with his right arm. "He's fine, Nat. Just a little shaken."

As soon as Aidan touched Natalie's fingers, she pulled him out of the water and crushed him to her chest.

Evan hauled himself out of the water once again and placed a hand on Nat's shoulder. "Like I said, he's fine."

"*This* time."

"Next time he falls into the water he needs to know how to handle himself."

Her eyes narrowed. "What's that supposed to mean?"

"He needs to take swimming lessons so he doesn't panic. Honestly, I'm surprised Coach hasn't started him yet."

"I'm his mother. I'll decide when he's ready for lessons."

"The earlier he starts, the easier it is. He doesn't want to be the only twelve-year-old in the tadpole class. I can teach him right here. Or even at the pool if that will make you feel more comfortable."

"You have no right to interfere."

"I'm his father—that gives me just as much right as you. We need to make decisions together that benefit Aidan, not encase him in a bubble."

"I'm protecting him."

"From what?"

"Getting hurt."

"Nat, pain is a great teacher."

"You don't need to tell me. I think we've had enough beach time for one day."

"Come on…"

She sighed. "I don't want to fight. Especially not here and not in front of Aidan."

With Aidan still in her arms, Natalie headed down the dock. At the blanket, she talked to Isabella, then started gathering their towels.

Exhaling loudly, Evan pulled himself out of the water and called the dogs. He trudged down the dock, the boards creaking beneath his feet.

One step forward, two steps back.

At some point, it had to get easier, right?

If not, then he had a long road ahead helping his son face his fears without his mother coddling him.

Evan was right.

And Natalie really hated admitting that.

Why did she react so badly around him?

Aidan needed to learn to swim, and she had to stop her own fears from holding him back.

As she peered through the narrow rectangular window in the door that led into the pool, Natalie couldn't help the smile that spread across her face as Aidan scrambled out of the water again and again to jump into Evan's open arms.

Each time Aidan did it, Evan praised him with as much enthusiasm as if it were the first time.

Yes, she really needed to let go because Evan was a great dad. She had been so wrong to deprive him of his son.

"He's doing a great job."

Natalie turned to find her father dressed in track pants and a light blue polo shirt with the activity center's logo embroidered on the left breast pocket. "Dad, what are you doing here, and why are you dressed for work?"

He shot her a very familiar grin. "Doc cleared me to go back to work. Part-time for now, but I can come in three days a week. Once swim season rolls around, I'll be as good as new."

"Are you sure that's a good idea? What does Mom say?"

Still smiling, he nodded. "We both think it's a good idea." He reached for her elbow and gave it a little tug. "Let's go outside and walk the track. I want to talk to you about something."

Natalie looked at her father, then cast a glance back through the pool door window just as Aidan popped up out of the water with the same excited expression he'd been wearing since Evan had coaxed him into the pool.

She longed to be in there with them, but she didn't want to interfere with Evan teaching their son how to swim.

"Natalie?"

She turned away from the window, then tightened her hold on Daisy's leash. "Coming. Daisy will enjoy the walk."

Hearing the *W* word, Daisy's ears perked. She started running ahead and pulling on the leash until Natalie stood still. When Daisy stopped tugging and waited, Natalie rewarded her with a treat and a head pat. "Good girl, Daisy. Let's walk."

Her father held the door as Natalie left the air-conditioned building and was smacked in the face by the midafternoon muggy August humidity. She moved her sunglasses off the top of her head and settled them on her face.

They strode down the sidewalk and pushed through the unlocked turnstile to the entrance of the field.

A couple of teenagers dressed in T-shirts and nylon running shorts ran past. They lifted a hand. "Hey, Coach."

He waved back. "Keep up the good work, guys."

She and her father fell in step while Daisy stayed by her side. "What did you want to talk about, Dad?"

"After the doctor cleared me to return to work, your mom and I went to lunch. We had a talk that was long overdue. As I mentioned the other day, my heart attack was a wake-up call for both of us. We're working too hard and pushing ourselves too much. It's time to slow down and enjoy more out of life than working long hours and coming home exhausted."

"Is Mom okay? She would have told me if she was sick, right?" Tightening her grip on Daisy's leash, Natalie's heart raced as she tried to recall her conversation with her mother before taking Aidan to meet Evan at the pool. She appeared to be in good health. If she lost her, what would she do?

Her father pressed a hand on Natalie's arm. "Stop. I can only imagine what you're thinking. Your mother is just fine."

Heat crawled across her cheeks. "Why do I always dive off into the deep end with my ridiculous thoughts?"

"They're not ridiculous. You just need to filter them so they offer truth and don't send you in a downward spiral. Anyway, your mom and I have looked at our schedules, and while we love what we do, we want to spend less time working and more time together."

"Are you talking retirement? Mom's only in her early fifties."

"Eventually, yes, but for now, we're going to cut our hours. Your mom cut back her hours at the clinic after my heart attack. Willow's been doing such a spectacular job that Mary's going to continue working those same hours. She's already talked to Willow about making her a partner instead of an associate."

"Willow won't let her down." Somehow Natalie couldn't picture her mother being content sitting at home while someone else ran her clinic, but she knew Willow would step up and do her mother proud.

"Definitely not. The doctor cleared me for coaching for three days a week, and when I'm able, I'll return to full-time through this year's swim season. Then I'm going to retire. Until you came home, we didn't think it was possible to take a step back from what we love. With the way you've been managing the kennel and even increased business, you've shown me it's time. I'd like to turn the business over to you, Natalie. It would give you the necessary place to expand and to grow your dog training."

"Dad, I don't know what to say."

"You don't have to say anything now. Think about it. Pray about it. Although I love working with the animals, my heart lies with coaching. I want to give them the best I have to offer before I retire."

"You've built the kennel business from the ground up. Do you really want to give that up? And what about coaching—who will take over?"

"I've given the board my coaching recommendation. I'm sure you'd agree with my choice. And don't you worry, Punky, I'll still be hanging around lending a hand with the kennel. But you've flourished over the past couple of months, and I'd really like to see what you can do. You can reestablish roots in Shelby Lake and be closer to those who love you."

Roots.

A secure home.

It was an answer to prayer.

The image of Evan's RV flashed into her thoughts.

Was she willing to put down roots in Shelby Lake if he wasn't sticking around? Or would she somehow be able to fight past her fears to have everything she'd always wanted—a secure home with the man she loved and the family they raised together? Even if it meant leaving Shelby Lake?

Chapter Twelve

More than anything, Evan wanted to say yes to the endorsement deal he'd been offered.

It was the opportunity of a lifetime. Not to mention the money he could put away for Aidan's future. But while his heart jumped to respond, his mouth had been slow to speak.

With the promise of giving an answer by the end of the week, Evan ended the call with his sports agent and cradled his head in his hands.

For the first time in his life, he had more than himself to consider. He had to think about how taking the endorsement opportunity would affect Aidan.

And Natalie.

How was he going to tell Natalie without her freaking out?

Lord, direct my steps. Show me the way You want me to go.

A glance at his watch showed he was going to be late picking up Natalie and Aidan.

To promote more family-friendly togetherness, Evan's church had put together a community event—Food and

Flix. Families were asked to bring chairs and blankets, and picnics to eat together. Then afterward, the church staff planned to have games and prizes. Once it grew darker, they were showing a family-friendly film on a makeshift outdoor screen and passing out popcorn.

When he'd pitched the idea to Natalie and invited her and Aidan to go, she had surprised him by saying yes.

Maybe he could find time to talk to her about the phone call he'd received.

If she said yes, then he'd be golden—not to mention having more money to put toward his house and maybe a little to tuck away for the future—their future.

Somehow he had to get her to say yes.

Less than twenty minutes later, he pulled into the Bishops' driveway behind Dr. Mary's parked sedan with the trunk open.

Coach came out the side door carrying a wicker picnic basket. Seeing Evan, he lifted a hand and stowed the basket in the trunk.

After cutting the engine, Evan pocketed his keys, hopped out and unhooked Toby from the back seat. Toby jumped down and stayed by Evan's side. "Hey, Coach. How's it goin'?"

"No complaints." He glanced at Evan and Toby, then back at Evan's truck. "No River?"

"Nah. Not tonight. He's hanging out on the farm. With Nat, Aidan and two dogs, I didn't have enough seat belts for all of us. Looks like I'm going to need a bigger vehicle to haul us around. Animals need to be secured, so if I'm going to continue with the fostering program, we'll need more room."

"Sounds like you're planning to stick around."

"We'll see what happens."

"You'll be okay without River?"

"I think so. The nightmares are lessening."

Smiling wide, Coach clapped him on the shoulder. "Glad to hear it."

The side door swung open and Aidan raced out, flinging his arms around Evan's legs. "Dad, Mom's being mean."

Detaching his son's arms from his legs, Evan knelt in front of the child. "What's going on?"

"She won't let me take my toys. She said they could get lost."

"Well, buddy, you need to listen to her. Your mom knows if they get lost, you'll be disappointed."

"If you say it's okay to take them, I can tell her yes. I can take them, right?"

Evan exchanged looks with Coach and smothered a laugh. "Dude, really? If your mom said no, I'm not going to say yes to make you happy. Then we'll both be in trouble. Besides, there's gonna to be so much other stuff to do."

"Fine." Aidan's bottom lip puffed out as he clasped his arms around his chest. Without another word, he trudged back to the house and slammed the door.

Evan pushed to his feet, and Coach slid an arm around his shoulders. "That's some pretty awesome parenting."

His mentor's words warmed him. "I'm no fool. Mom's word is law. I can't blame him for trying, though. I'm sure I did the same thing when I was a kid."

"And how'd that work for you."

"About as well as it did for Aidan."

Twenty minutes later, after getting everyone loaded and buckled in, they pulled into the church parking lot.

Evan's brothers arrived right behind them with their families.

Evan unfolded a plaid blanket and spread it on the ground behind Tucker, Isabella and the twins, and between his father and Claudia and Jake and Tori.

Coach and Dr. Mary settled on the other side of Evan's father and Claudia.

Natalie opened her picnic basket and pulled out a blue plastic rectangular container, two matching covered plastic bowls and a smaller rectangular container. "I wasn't sure what you'd like but I made chicken bacon ranch wraps, pasta salad, cut-up fruit and blackberry crumb bars."

"Man, that sounds great. You didn't have to go to all of this trouble. You could've asked me to grab a pizza or something on the way over."

Pink stole across her cheeks. Her ponytail fell forward, veiling her face. He longed to tuck it back where it belonged, but he kept his hands to himself.

"I enjoyed doing it."

They made their plates and chatted with their families around them while they ate.

After finishing a second helping, Evan stretched out on his back with his right arm behind his head. He patted his stomach and sighed. "Tank's full."

Aidan stretched out beside him and patted his own stomach. "My tank's full, too."

Evan grinned and cupped an arm around his son.

"Too bad you're full. I also made chocolate chip cookies as a surprise." Natalie pulled out another plastic container, lifted up the corner of the lid, and the scents of sugar, vanilla and chocolate wafted toward them.

Leaning up on his elbow, Evan raised an eyebrow. "I'm sure I can find room for a cookie or two."

"Me, too." Aidan sat up and grabbed a cookie from the container. "Can I take one to Livie and Landon?"

"Sure, go ahead." Natalie wrapped a couple of cookies in a napkin and handed them to him.

Taking the cookies, Aidan scrambled off the blanket and headed toward his cousins. "Hey, guys. Guess what?"

Evan sat up. "If I lie here, I'm going to fall into a food coma. Want to take a walk?"

Natalie looked at him, then cast a glance at Aidan sharing cookies with Livie and Landon.

He pressed a hand to her arm. "He'll be fine. We'll take a quick walk around the block and be back before the movie starts. Besides, I want to talk to you about something."

She nodded. "Okay, I want to talk to you about something, too."

After being reassured by Tucker and Isabella they had no problem keeping an eye on Aidan, Natalie pushed to her feet and brushed crumbs off her flowered skirt. Paired with a pink T-shirt and white sandals, she was the epitome of summertime.

Evan wanted to take her hand, but he didn't want to pressure her, especially in front of a crowd of people.

Once they rounded the corner and were out of view of the church, Evan took her hand. "What did you want to talk to me about?"

"Dad and I had a good talk the other day while you were in the pool with Aidan."

"Yeah? What about?"

"His doctor released him to return to work part-time."

"That's good news."

"Yes, it is. I think it will help him get some of his energy back, too. But he said his heart attack was a wake-up call. He and Mom are cutting back their hours. Mom's promoting Willow from associate to partner at the clinic."

"Even more good news. Willow will do a dynamite job."

"No doubt. When Dad had his heart attack, Mom cut her hours, and she's going to keep those same hours. Even though Dad's coaching only three days a week for now, he'd like to return full-time...until he retires in the spring."

"Whoa, Coach is retiring? He's a legend. Who'll take his place? Will he run the kennels full-time?"

"Dad gave a recommendation to the board for a re-placement." Natalie faced Evan. "I probably shouldn't say anything and Dad didn't come out and say it, but he alluded to the fact that he suggested your name."

"Me? I'm no coach."

The idea of following in Coach's footsteps seemed a little overwhelming, but like Nat said, he may not have been who Coach referred.

"No, but you love the water, and you've been doing an excellent job working with Aidan. But again, I may be speaking out of turn. As far as the kennels go, Dad wants to retire from those, too. He said he doesn't mind lending a hand, but he asked me to take over the busi-ness. Not only could I continue with the boarding side of it, but I would have a place to establish my dog training business here in Shelby Lake. I could keep partnering with Zoe Sullivan to grow the service dog project. And Willow and I would like to work with the school district to bring in dogs to help children with reading challenges to grow their skills and confidence."

He needed to be excited for Nat, and he was. He hadn't seen her this animated since returning home.

He forced enthusiasm into his voice. "You're sure excited about this, Nat."

A wide smile spread across her face. "I am. I've been thinking about it for the past few days. I wanted to talk about it with you because it does affect Aidan indirectly. Once your family agreed to the service dog program at the beginning of the month, I gave notice to my aunt that we were moving. Aidan's really flourished this summer, and I feel like we can put down roots in Shelby Lake." She waved a hand in front of her face. "I'm sorry. I've been going on and on without giving you any time to speak. What did you want to talk to me about?"

He brushed away her question. "Eh, that can wait. I'm really happy for you. It sounds like this is the kind of opportunity you've been waiting for."

"It could be an answer to prayer." She lifted a shoulder and raised her eyes to him. "I don't know. Maybe God hasn't forgotten me after all."

"I don't doubt that for a moment."

"Thank you, Evan, for being so patient with me. For believing in me. Even though the idea of taking over Dad's business scares me a little, I remembered what you told Aidan about being courageous. So I'm trying to find the courage to move forward with my life and not allow my past to hold me back." She stood on tiptoe, and kissed him.

He wrapped her in his arms and breathed in her essence. Even though he was excited for her newfound enthusiasm, he realized he was in the position where he was going to have to choose between Natalie and chasing after his own dreams.

Unfortunately, there wouldn't be a middle ground between the two.

Tucker and Isabella made falling in love look so easy.

In the short time Natalie had gotten to know the bride, she'd learned it had been anything but easy for the two childhood friends who'd reunited last year—the widowed single father and the insecure chef who struggled with abandonment issues.

Something Natalie could totally relate to.

When Isabella had returned to Shelby Lake after losing her prestigious job, she'd stayed to help save her father's diner and care for Tucker's children after his nanny quit. Despite their ups and downs, their story was what romance novels were made of.

And now Natalie had been invited to see them get married.

Natalie and Aidan sat next to her parents in the right section of pews in the sanctuary of the Shelby Lake Community Church. Sunlight streamed through the stained-glass windows, scattering jewels of light across the ruby-colored carpet.

Peach and white roses had been attached to the mint-green and white bows at the end of the pews. Dressed in matching mint-green sleeveless dresses, Isabella's best friend, Jeanne, and Jake's wife, Tori, made their way down the aisle as Alec Seaver played a romantic song on his guitar.

Landon, dressed in a gray tux, carried a small pillow and walked beside Olivia, who wore a peach dress and scattered a trail of rose petals on the dove-gray aisle runner.

As they passed by Natalie's pew, Landon waved. "Hi, Aidan."

The small gathering of close friends and family laughed quietly.

The music tempo changed and Isabella appeared in the doorway holding on to her father's arm. As everyone stood, Natalie's gasp joined the chorus of the others.

Dressed in a white lacy off-the-shoulder gown with a sweetheart neckline and beaded bodice that emphasized Isabella's tiny waist, and a full skirt with beaded lace appliqués, she looked like a princess, especially with the long veil that was attached to her updo and swept along behind her.

Natalie stole a glance at Tucker.

Hands clasped in front of him, he stood tall and composed, wearing a grin only a man in love could pull off. His lovestruck gaze didn't waver as he watched his bride come toward him.

Jake and Evan stood next to him. Micah hadn't been able to make it, much to the family's disappointment.

Natalie's heart sighed.

A true romance.

Would she have that?

Could she have it with Evan?

They'd been growing closer since the night at the escape room, but since last weekend's movie night at Evan's church, he'd seemed a little distant again.

Or maybe her insecurities were feeding her vivid imagination.

For the first time in years, Natalie considered that

having her own happily-ever-after might be possible after all.

The freedom that created within her sent an unexpected rush of tears to her eyes. She tried to blink them back, but one managed to trickle down her cheek.

As she traced it away with the back of her pinkie, Natalie looked up to find Evan watching her with an endearing expression. He winked, which sent her pulse skidding.

Her eyes roamed over the way his gray tux jacket hugged his wide shoulders. She had been so used to him being in T-shirts, and shorts or jeans, that seeing him in a well-fitted suit stole her breath.

Once Joe, Isabella's father, had given her over to Tucker, the pastor invited the guests to sit.

For the next twenty minutes, Tucker and Isabella made promises to each other, pledged their love and sealed it with a kiss, eliciting cheering from the guests and whistles from Jake and Evan.

After the ceremony, Natalie waited outside the church with Aidan and her parents for the bride and groom to make their exit.

Moments later, Tucker and Isabella rushed down the wide steps through a gale of bubbles dancing and floating in the breeze instead of the usual tossed rice.

Someone touched her elbow. She turned to find Evan standing so close that the subtle outdoorsy scent of his cologne enveloped her. At that moment, she wanted nothing more than to wrap her arms around his neck and pull him close.

But she couldn't do that.

At least not there.

Instead, she pasted on a smile, thankful for being able

to hide behind her sunglasses, and brushed her hand over his sleeve. "Hey. You clean up nice. It was a beautiful wedding, wasn't it?"

"Thanks." Evan's eyes darkened as his gaze roamed over her burgundy floral wrap dress. "Yes, it was. Tucker and Isabella deserve a lifetime of happiness. And speaking of beautiful, you look gorgeous."

She couldn't fight the heat that warmed her cheeks so she looked away, toying with the snap on her clutch purse. "Thanks."

Someone called his name, and he lifted his hand in acknowledgment. "I have to head back inside for pictures. See you at the reception?"

She nodded, not trusting her voice.

Once he left her side, she felt strangely alone. Silly, since her parents were less than a foot away and the front churchyard was filled with people.

After she managed to pull her parents away from their conversations with half the guests, they headed up Holland Hill for a rustic picnic reception honoring Tucker and Isabella's first date, complete with a taco bar and s'mores for dessert.

A large canopy tent covered at least a dozen banquet tables arranged in three rows and pushed together for family-style seating. White cloths covered the tables, along with mint-green place mats and matching runners. Clusters of peach and white roses in shallow bowls with clear gems lined the middle. Swags of tiny lights swathed in mint-colored tulle draped from the canopy ceiling poles, scattering tiny gems of light across the reception area.

Off to the side, under a smaller canopy, a DJ had set up a stage with a makeshift dance floor.

For the next hour, Natalie tried to keep Aidan seated so he would eat and not run off to play with Livie and Landon, who were bouncing in their chairs at the bridal table. Friends chatted with her and her parents. While she tried to pay attention to conversations, her focus kept drifting toward Evan, especially when Aidan escaped and raced over to his father, sitting next to Jake.

Having shed his jacket, Evan rolled up the sleeves to his dress shirt, exposing his tanned, muscular forearms, and undid his tie. He lifted Aidan in his lap and laughed at something the boy whispered in his ear. Evan caught her eye and winked, said something to Aidan, and then they left the table as the DJ invited the bride and groom to the dance floor.

Tucker drew Isabella close, whispered something in her ear, and as wedding guests clinked their silverware against their glasses, he lowered his head and kissed her sweetly, eliciting sounds of "aww" from the crowd.

Someone placed hands on Natalie's shoulders, and she didn't need to turn to know Evan was behind her. He whispered in her ear, "Dance with me."

It wasn't a question. But he didn't even need to ask.

She smiled, then held out her hand. He took it in his and led her to the dance floor, where his hands settled on her waist. She curled her arms around his neck and moved along with his graceful steps.

She belonged in his arms, and it was time to stop lying to herself about it.

Resting her cheek against him, she listened to the low rumble in his chest as he sang along with the lyrics, serenading her quietly.

She sighed.

"What's wrong?"

Evan's words, spoken quietly, nudged one of those bricks in her wall.

How could she tell him she was falling in love with him all over again? What if he didn't feel the same way? Or worse, what if he hadn't forgiven her yet?

The underlying thread of anxiety and fear that made her question everything could be tugged at the wrong moment, causing her happiness to unravel.

She shook her head.

Evan pulled back and tipped up her chin. "Why don't I believe you?"

"I'm fine. Really."

"Would you still be fine if I kissed you right now?"

She darted a look around the yard, then back at him. "I don't think that would be a good idea."

"I think kissing you is the best idea I've had today." Evan brushed a thumb over her cheek.

"Not here. Not in front of everyone."

He grinned. "So if we were somewhere else, you'd let me kiss you?"

How was she supposed to answer that?

She rested her head against Evan's chest and allowed the words to a romantic song about finding love again wash over her. When the music ended, they broke apart. Not letting go of her hand, Evan guided her off the dance floor. "Let's get out of here. I need you to myself for a bit."

"Hey, you two leaving?" They turned to find Jake and Tori, hand in hand, heading to the dance floor.

"Hey, man. No, we're…uh…going for a walk…to talk."

"Talk, huh? Yeah, a walk's great for that." Jake's smirk sent a rush of heat to Natalie's cheeks.

"Leave them alone." Tori batted at her husband's chest, then she smiled at them. "Hey, Ev. With all the wedding prep going on this week, I haven't congratulated you on the endorsement deal."

Natalie's eyes zipped to Evan's. "What endorsement deal?"

Tori's eyes widened as her mouth formed an O. She gave Evan a pained look and mouthed, *Sorry.*

Evan wrapped an arm around her shoulder and directed her toward the road. "Let's take a walk."

Suddenly she had the feeling the walk wouldn't have anything to do with the alone time he had been imagining between them.

Once they were out of earshot, Natalie turned, shrugging off Evan's arm. "What was Tori talking about?"

"I've been offered an endorsement opportunity."

"I see. Were you planning to tell me?"

"Yes, of course. I wanted to tell you when we attended the Food and Flix event at church, but you were so excited about taking over Coach's business that I didn't want to rain on your parade."

"I've seen you every day since, but you haven't said a word, Evan. What kind of endorsement deal?"

"It's for a travel website promoting different activities at a popular beach resort. If I accept, I'll be highlighting their different paddle sports—canoeing, kayaking, stand-up paddleboards. Basically, I'd need to go and film a commercial."

"Then what?"

"Then…I come home and deposit the check in the savings account I've started for Aidan's future."

"No, Ev. What happens after this endorsement? What if you're offered another? And another?"

Evan lifted his shoulders. "I can't predict the future, Nat. I have no idea what's going to happen. I may mess things up and no one will want to touch me. I just have to put it in God's hands and go from there."

"What if this puts you back on the water? Or has you traveling all over the place? Aidan needs a father who is going to be there for him. Not someone who flies in and out of his life when it's convenient."

A muscle jumped along the curve of his jaw as his brows furrowed. "I'm not like that, and you know it. I honor my responsibilities. And this opportunity could help save for Aidan's future. If I decide to do it, both of you could come with me. We could turn it into a family vacation."

Her jaw tightened. "Aidan starts school next week. And I've told you, I don't want a lifetime on the road, not having roots."

"We're not talking a lifetime, Nat. This is a one-time gig. Short term."

"I'm sorry, Evan. I just can't."

"Can't or won't? Why does everything have to be so black-and-white with you?"

"Because shades of gray lead to heartbreak. I just feel like once won't be enough for you. I saw you in action, remember? I saw that adrenaline rush, that winner's high. How will this be different?"

"This isn't me competing. It's being in one commercial spot that will be aired online. This has nothing to do with my career."

"Of course it does. You were offered this gig because you're a great paddler. They wouldn't want you if you were a nobody, Evan. You just can't see yourself as others do. You're blinded by a mistake that makes you feel like a failure."

"How do *you* see me?"

"What?"

"You heard me. I want to know how you see me."

"Why does that matter?"

"Because it matters to me."

She turned away and wrapped her arms around her waist. "I see you as someone who is strong and brave. You have the ability to overcome difficulties and reach for your dreams. You're a great father to Aidan. And a good friend to me."

"That's it? You see me as just a friend? Nothing more?"

"Yes, a friend, because anything else is just too painful."

Just once, why couldn't she be truthful? To him. And to herself.

Evan slid his hand behind her neck and put his other hand around her waist, pulling her close. "No, Nat, you're wrong. I can be your friend. And so much more. We can be great together if you just give us a chance."

Tears filled her eyes and blurred her vision. "I can't. Don't you see—it's not just about me anymore. I have to think about Aidan. What if we get involved again and it doesn't work out? It's not just my heart that's in pieces all over again. I have a little boy to consider."

"Why are you expecting me to break your heart?"

"Because we…" She swept an arm over the land. "This isn't enough for you. Like I've said before—river water runs in your veins. The water calls to you."

"No, Nat. It doesn't. Maybe at one time, yes, it did. Even though I've been following my passion, I've realized since I've been home there's been something missing right here." He pressed a fist to his chest. "I want more. I want a family. I want someone who is willing to go through life with me, cheer me on through the difficulties and not give up on me. I want to be worth someone's time and effort."

Say it. Say you can be that person.

Even though her head wanted her to speak up, her heart forced her to stay silent.

He took a step back and scraped a hand over his face, his eyes suspiciously wet. "I have a feeling that no matter how much I love you and tell you how I feel, it's not going to be enough. You're so blinded by the pain of your past that you're not willing to risk your heart for someone whose words means something. I don't know what I have to do to prove I'm worth being in your life, being a good dad to Aidan, but I can't keep jerking my heart around hoping that maybe someday you'll be brave enough to take a chance. I hope you can find what you're looking for, Natalie. But apparently it's not with me."

Evan brushed his lips across her forehead and, without another glance, walked away.

Balling her hands into fists, Natalie clamped her jaw tight and forced the shudder in her chest to keep her from melting into a puddle on the side of the country road.

Chapter Thirteen

If she could turn back time, she'd go back to the day before Chuck Holland's birthday party when she and Willow had talked about partnering with Zoe and the Hollands on the service dog project and say she wasn't interested. She'd come up with an excuse to avoid taking her father to the cookout.

Then she wouldn't have run into Evan.

She wouldn't have spent the past month falling in love with him all over again. And she wouldn't be spending her evenings crying into her pillow like a lovesick teenager.

Running the back of her hand over her cheeks, Natalie stepped out of the dress she had bought for the wedding and kicked it into the bottom of her closet, knowing she could never wear it again without remembering the brokenness in Evan's eyes before he'd walked away from her.

After pulling on a purple T-shirt and a pair of old jeans with holes in the knees, Natalie dried her face with the hem of her shirt, slipped her feet into a pair of black flip-flops, then headed downstairs and outside to the kennels.

Spending time with the dogs would soothe her wounded spirit.

Her mother's car wasn't in the garage, so the rest of her family were still at the wedding. When she pleaded a headache and wanted to leave, they'd offered to bring Aidan home. She was more than happy to let him stay. She didn't want to deal with a meltdown when she pulled him away from his cousins.

She went into the kennel kitchen and started getting the dogs' dinner bowls ready. She had portioned out their food after breakfast, so all she had to do was drop it into clean bowls, mix in wet food for the dogs who needed it and cart their meals to their suites. She exchanged her flip-flops for the pair of paw-print rain boots she wore for cleaning up after the animals.

Bert, a long-faced basset hound, met her at the door of his suite, his tail wagging. She unhinged his door, petted him a moment, then swapped out his empty dish from that morning with a bowl filled with his kibble. She gave him fresh water, backed out and relocked the door so he would eat.

She stopped at the next suite, where Buster the beagle was curled up in his bed in the corner. As a first-time visitor, he wasn't used to the noise from the other dogs. He slunk low to meet her at the door with his ears pinned back. She sat on the floor while he crawled into her lap so she could rub his belly. Then she gave him fresh food and water.

By the time she'd delivered the rest of the food dishes, Bert had finished eating. She hooked his leash to his collar and led him outside to the play yard so she could clean and disinfect his suite.

By keeping busy and focusing on the animals, maybe she wouldn't have time to rewind Evan's words and replay them in her head for the hundredth time.

He loved her.

Not the way she'd wanted to hear those words, but still, he'd said them.

And she was the jerk who threw them to the ground and stomped all over them.

No wonder he'd walked away.

When would it end? The constant fear and anxiety that kept her from moving forward, from reaching for what she wanted.

From the driveway, car doors slammed, sending the dogs into a barking frenzy.

Everyone was home.

After scrubbing Bert's suite with a long-handed scrub brush, she rinsed the floor and sprayed disinfectant. Then she retrieved clean bedding, rinsed the floor once again, replaced his bedding and refreshed his water.

She knew these tasks by heart and could practically do them in her sleep.

She repeated the process for the remaining suites. By the time she had thrown the dirty bedding in the washer and portioned out the dogs' meals for the next day, she was ready for a hot shower and to crawl into bed.

But she couldn't bury her head under her pillow just yet.

The laundry would need to be changed over and the dogs taken back outside one last time.

With a storm brewing, she'd probably sneak out to check on them, especially the ones afraid of the thunder.

Then maybe she could crash for the night and put this miserable day behind her.

She'd just finished showering and changing into yoga pants and a clean T-shirt when a knock sounded on her bedroom door. Without waiting for a response, the door opened and her mother walked in, still wearing the navy dress printed with daisies that she'd worn to the wedding. "Can I come in?"

Natalie nodded as she unwound her wet hair from the towel.

"How's your headache?"

Natalie balled the towel in her hands and sat on the edge of the bed, her eyes filling with tears once again. She buried her face in the wet towel and sobbed.

Mom moved from the open doorway and sat next to her, tucking her wet hair behind her ear. She wrapped an arm around her shoulder. "Oh, honey. Is it that bad? Can I get you anything?"

She shook her head and wiped her face. Swallowing past the boulder in her throat, Natalie told her mother about the conversation with Evan. "I ruined everything, Mom."

"It may seem that way now, but I'm sure you two can work things out."

She shook her head, rubbing a hand over her forehead to ease the ache forming for real this time. "He left. He walked away."

"Give him time."

"Part of me wants to pack up and leave."

Next to her room, Aidan's door slammed.

Had he been listening to their conversation?

She waited to see if she could hear anything else from

his room. Just to be sure, Natalie slipped off the bed and closed her door.

"Why?"

"So I don't have to see him again."

"Natalie Grace, that's your broken heart talking. You don't mean that. Aidan's looking forward to going to school with Livie and Landon next week. And he's getting to know his father. You don't want to take him away from all of that simply because life is hard right now. You have to come to a point in your life when you're done running." Mom took her hands. "Let go of the past and embrace your future."

"I don't even know how to do that."

"Give it up to God."

"How do I hand twenty-plus years of anxiety over to God?" Natalie cradled her head in her hands.

Mom started rubbing her back. "Oh, honey, it's definitely a process. When I moved back to Shelby Lake, I was full of shame for my choices and the resulting consequences that created trauma for you and Ben. My parents were so supportive. God forgave me, but I struggled with forgiving myself. I had married the wrong man and nearly lost my precious children. Then, I met Ted, who taught me about God's unconditional love. Not just through his words, but through his actions, too. It's a process that takes time, trust and grace."

A knock sounded on her door. Mom crossed the room and opened it. Dad stood in the doorway with a tired look on his face.

"What's wrong, Ted?"

"Aidan's gone."

Natalie pushed off the bed. "What do you mean gone?"

"I went upstairs to see if he wanted ice cream, but his room was empty. His sneakers and backpack are missing."

Ice coursed through her veins. Her fingers trembled and her heart quaked. "It's getting dark and there's a storm coming. We need to find him." Natalie tried to push past her father, but he reached for her arms and turned her to face him. "Call Evan and let him know what's going on. He can help with the search."

Her stomach cinched in knots, Natalie checked around her room but her phone wasn't in sight. Then she remembered her jeans from cleaning the kennels. After pulling it out of the back pocket, she scrolled through her phone and tapped on his name.

The phone rang, but he didn't pick up. He probably saw her name on the screen and hit Ignore. Getting his voice mail, she forced her voice to remain calm, explained the situation and asked him to call back as soon as possible.

She gripped the silent phone as she shoved her bare feet into flip-flops and headed out the door into the fading daylight.

She lifted her eyes to the darkening sky and uttered, "God, protect my little boy."

Evan had no idea how things had fallen apart so quickly.

One minute they'd been searching for a quiet spot to connect, then after Tori's accidental spill about the endorsement deal, Natalie had shut down.

Despite baring his heart, it hadn't been enough. Knowing he wouldn't have been able to change her mind and not wanting to cause a scene that ruined his brother's wedding day, Evan had walked away.

Maybe he should have stayed.

Maybe they could've talked things out.

But with the set of her jaw, Evan knew she'd made her mind up already.

Maybe tomorrow would be different. He didn't know. Right now, though, he wanted to help with cleanup, then hole up in the RV with the dogs and hope tomorrow was a better day.

After Tucker and Isabella left for their honeymoon, his father and Claudia had herded the overly tired, hyped-on-sugar twins back to the farmhouse for baths and bed.

Evan changed out of his tux and then helped Jake, who had done the same, to tear down tables and chairs and put away the tents.

As he stacked the folding chairs borrowed from the church, his thoughts spun back to the anger on Natalie's face.

Man, he hated the drama of relationships.

He added the last chair to the back of the pickup with a little more force than necessary.

"Whoa, dude, take it easy. What's up with you?" Jake rounded the truck with a black trash bag in his hand. He tossed it over the side, landing it next to the last stack of chairs.

"I'm fine." Evan pulled an empty trash bag off the roll in the front of the truck and picked up stray forks, balled-up napkins and empty bubble bottles.

"Yeah, you look it."

Evan leaned against the bed of the farm truck. "Natalie and I had a fight."

"About what?"

Evan lifted a shoulder. "We want different things, I guess."

"I'm sorry, dude. That's messed up. Maybe things will be different tomorrow. Sleep has a way of clearing away anger." Jake grabbed a couple of waters out of the leftover tub of beverages and handed one to Evan. "Still blows my mind that you have a kid."

"Yeah, you and me both, man. Aidan's a great kid. Every time he calls me Dad my heart bumps against my ribs." Evan nudged his brother. "A couple more months, then you can join Tuck and me in fatherhood."

A grin split Jake's face. "Can't wait. That leaves Micah. You hear from him lately?"

"About a week ago or so. He said he'd be here for the wedding. Then he texted Tuck and said something came up and he wouldn't be able to make it."

"What could be more important than family?"

"Cut Micah some slack, okay? The past few years haven't been easy on him."

"They haven't been easy on any of us. That's why we stick together—to help each other through those tough times. That's what family does."

"Yeah, well, sometimes we tend to rely on ourselves instead of being a burden to others."

"Micah wouldn't be a burden." Jake swept a hand over the property. "We started the Fatigues to Farming program to help veterans like him—to give them a sense of hope and a purpose so they won't camp out on park benches."

Evan held up his hands. "Hey, man. I believe you. You're doing a fine job, but as Coach used to tell me— you gotta want to change to make it happen."

"Ain't that the truth." Jake clinked his plastic bottle against Evan's.

"Let's talk about something that's not going to get you all twisted up inside. Do you know what you're having yet?"

"No, Tori wants to be surprised, so no gender reveal for us. Either way, we're excited for a healthy baby."

"You pick out names?"

One more thing he'd missed out on doing during Nat's pregnancy.

"Yeah, but Tori's been pretty tight-lipped about what we've chosen. She wants them to be a surprise. If I tell you, don't say anything."

Evan held up two fingers. "Scout's honor."

"If it's a boy, he'll be named Charles Jacob and we'll call him Charlie."

"Cute. Dad will love that."

"Yeah, we thought so. If it's a girl, her name will be Lillian Christina, and we'll call her Lilly."

"Mom's first name and Claudia's middle name. Nice." Evan drained his bottle of water, pitched it into the trash bag and glanced at the darkening sky. "We need to work quickly to get everything torn down and loaded before the rain hits."

They slid the last table into the bed of Jake's truck. After pulling up stakes and tearing down the tents rented for the reception, Jake and Evan bagged the poles. They folded the material and stacked everything on top of the borrowed banquet tables to be returned to the church.

Claudia's cherry-red SUV shot up the drive and braked next to the farm truck. Their father opened the door and hurried out, his face creased in deep lines. "You two knuckleheads forget how to answer a phone?"

Jake pulled his out of his back pocket and waved it. "Sorry, Pops. My volume's been off since the wedding."

Evan patted his shorts pockets. "I must have left mine in my tux pants pocket. What's going on?"

"Ted called. Natalie's been trying to get a hold of you. Aidan's gone missing."

Evan froze. "What do you mean gone missing? How long ago was that?"

Dad glanced at his watch. "About twenty minutes ago."

Off in the distance, heat lightning stroked the sky.

"A storm's rolling in sooner than expected." Evan dragged a hand over his face. "We need to split up and find him. Dad, can you run me back so I can grab my truck?"

"Hop in. Jake, head down the hill and trace the route from the Bishops' to Joe's Diner. I'll take the other end of the hill near the Watsons' and work my way back to our place. Ev, run along the property line. Let's find him before the rain hits."

Evan rounded the SUV and slammed the door just as the sky opened and rain bulleted the windshield.

So much for the rain holding off.

With the wipers squeegeeing the water from the glass, Evan mumbled the same prayer over and over. "God, please protect my son."

Back at his place, Evan scrounged through his tux for his phone, dug through a duffel for rain gear, then hustled outside to his truck.

He slid in behind the wheel and started the engine. "Guide me, God."

As he drove at a snail's pace down the road, Evan

tried to scan the fields for his little boy, but between the darkness and falling rain, visibility was nearly invisible.

How was he going to find Aidan in this downpour?

He was not going to let negative thinking affect his focus or feed his fears.

Hopefully, Aidan was about to find shelter out of the storm. He could only imagine how scared the little boy would be once the thunder and lightning struck.

After driving slowly up and down the main road along the Holland property and seeing nothing, Evan braked and pressed his head against the rest.

He needed to think.

Where would the little guy have gone?

A sudden image of the footbridge over the stream flashed before his eyes.

Throwing the truck in Reverse, Evan backed up the truck to the narrow, rutted lane between the cornfield and pasture that led to Arrowhead Creek.

At the end of the path, he cut through the grassy area and stopped at the bank. He shut off the engine, leaving the headlights on so he could see. Evan shrugged on a rain jacket and grabbed a floatable flashlight from the glove box. He patted his back pocket to make sure he had his phone this time.

Still wearing his flip-flops, he slid in the wet grass as he rounded the truck to search the steep bank. He meant to grab his wet shoes but he had been so focused on hurrying to find Aidan that he left the RV without them. And now he didn't want to waste the time to go back and get them. He'd have to make the best of it.

Shining his light over the footbridge, he found it empty, but the bridge wasn't in the same spot. He moved the light closer. It looked like it had been moved.

"Aidan!" The wind picked up, grabbing his words and carrying them away.

Evan scrambled down the bank, his feet sliding in the mud. He kicked off his flip-flops, hoping he'd have better traction with his bare feet.

He scanned the bank with the light. "Aidan!"

The rain pounding against the rocks and the rushing water drowned out any sound.

Please, God...

At the base of the bank, he slipped the flashlight under his arm and cupped his hands around his mouth. "Aidan!"

Still nothing.

Evan turned to check the creek on the other side of the footbridge. As he tried to climb around the footbridge, his foot slipped, and he slammed his left shoulder into the wood. He bit back a howl and tried to stand. His flashlight dropped into the water and floated under the bridge.

Icy water slid over his bare skin and rocks cut into his feet as he surged for the light. He lost his footing again, falling into the water, and the flashlight floated out of reach.

Thunder crashed and lightning speared the sky.

A scream sounded not too far from Evan, on the other side of the creek. His pulse raced as a surge of adrenaline pushed him to his feet. "Aidan!"

Using the bridge as a guide, Evan sloshed through the water and ducked under the wooden platform. His foot caught on something.

Probably a fallen branch from one of the overhead trees.

He reached down to free it. Instead of tree bark, he

touched vinyl. He tugged and lifted a sodden backpack out of the water. From the glare of the truck headlights, he could make out a Spider-Man logo.

Aidan's backpack.

Chest heaving and heart racing, Evan threw it up on the bank. He kept one hand against the bank and walked slowly down the creek bed. "Aidan!"

"Dad!"

Relief washed over him. "Aidan, I'm coming. Listen for my voice."

"I'm stuck."

"I'm coming, buddy. Keep talking."

Evan hurried toward the sound of his son's voice. He tried to make out a shape or something that would alert him to Aidan's location, but with the tree cover, darkness and the rain, he was walking blindly.

His foot hit a protruding rock. He scrambled to break his fall. He pitched forward, his shoulder slamming again into the water, this time against a log or something.

He felt a familiar pop, along with blades of fire that sliced from his elbow to his neck. He let out a moan as bile rose in his throat. He tried to shift his body to his right to gain momentum, but his knee slid on an algae-covered rock, causing him to lose his balance and fall face-first into the water.

Holding his left arm tightly to his chest, he pushed his right hand against the bottom of the creek bed and managed to move to his knees. "Aidan, I'm coming." His voice sounded garbled, strangled to his own ears.

Fire blazed in his shoulder joint as water splashed over him.

His heartbeat thundered in his ears. Sweat slicked his

skin. Pressure ballooned in his chest. His ragged breathing came in shallow breaths.

He was trapped. Caught. The water. The darkness.

He tugged on the collar of his soaked T-shirt, trying to make room to breathe.

"Dad!"

Evan sucked in a lungful of air mixed with pelting rain. "C-coming, A-Aidan."

Mustering as much strength as he could, Evan gritted his teeth and pushed to his feet, letting out a growl.

"Dad! What was that?"

"It's okay, buddy. Where are you?"

"I'm in a tree in the water."

"Hang tight, I'm coming. Keep talking." Evan plodded through the water, his feet numb, his legs scraped and battered.

"I caught something." A moment later, a light flicked on. "A flashlight, Dad. Can you see me?"

Realizing Aidan was only about five feet ahead of him, Evan could have wept.

But first he needed to save his son.

He powered forward, slipping and sliding, but still standing.

A moment later, he reached Aidan, who was waist deep in the water, clinging to a small, fallen tree.

Evan reached for him and tugged the boy to his chest, but his leg wouldn't move.

"My foot is stuck."

Evan ran his hand down the outside of Aidan's leg and felt for his foot. He slipped his shoe off, and Aidan's foot slid free. He wrapped his arms around Evan's neck. "You saved me, Dad. I knew you'd find me."

Still holding Aidan's shoe, Evan pulled his arm free

of the tree branches and wrapped Aidan tightly against his chest.

With Aidan's arms and legs wrapped around Evan, they slowly made their way back to the footbridge. Aidan held the flashlight so they could see where they were going.

Evan slipped, but he managed to keep a tight hold on his son. Once they reached the footbridge, Evan released Aidan on the worn wood. He reached for his phone in his back pocket, but it was missing. It must've slipped out when Evan took his first fall. He eyed the bank, which looked more like Mount Everest. "Buddy, you need to listen to me, okay?"

Evan brushed Aidan's wet hair out of his face as he nodded. "Remember how I said superheroes go through a lot of tough stuff to make them strong and brave?"

Aidan nodded again. "Like you, Dad. You're a superhero. You saved me."

"No, buddy, you were the strong and brave one. Even though it's wet, I need you to put your shoe back on and run back to your house and get Mommy or Grandpa, okay? Can you do that for me?"

"But it's dark, and I'm scared." Shivering, Aidan pulled his knees to his chest and wrapped his arms around his legs.

Evan tapped his son's chest. "You are strong and brave. Courage comes from here, remember? Take my flashlight and run superfast back to Grandpa's. Bring him back here. I hurt my shoulder, and I can't climb the bank. The footbridge won't hold me. Please, Aidan, I know you can do this."

With a fearful look etched on his face, Aidan picked up the shoe off the bridge and put it on. Then, holding on to the flashlight, he stood. The bridge teetered and Aidan pitched forward. "Dad!"

Evan caught him before he fell into the water. He righted the bridge. "I'll hold it steady while you hurry across, okay?"

"Okay, Dad." Without another word, Aidan scrambled to his feet again and ran across the bridge onto the grass. He jumped and waved his arms like a champion. "I did it."

"I knew you could. Go get Grandpa!"

Evan watched as the light bobbed and bounced down the grassy trail until it was out of sight. With rain pelting his face, he lay against the bank and forced his breathing to calm.

Aidan was safe.

Thank you, God.

Chapter Fourteen

Ring. Please ring.

Natalie sat on the edge of the couch and stared at the phone, waiting for word from someone, anyone, to let her know Aidan had been found.

It remained silent.

Daisy rested beside her, and Alice was curled up at her feet.

Her mother came into the living room carrying two steaming mugs. "I made you some tea. You can hold the cup instead of your phone."

"What if they don't find him? What if he's out in the storm all night long?"

"They will find him. Half the county is looking for him. Keep praying and trust God to bring him home safely."

So much easier said than done.

Natalie took a sip of peppermint tea and forced herself not to look at her phone.

The clock hanging on the wall over the couch ticked loudly. Too loudly.

Most days, the TV was on, Aidan was running

through the house and dogs were barking, so she wasn't used to this stillness.

Except late at night when everyone else was in bed.

After waking up from a nightmare, she'd creep downstairs, turn the TV on low and curl up on the couch, trying to block out the images that roused her from sleep.

If they couldn't find her son…

No, she wasn't going there. She needed to hold on to hope.

Hands cupped around her tea, her mother rested her head against the back of the couch and closed her eyes. Her lips moved silently.

She was praying.

What would it be like to have a faith like that? No matter what challenges you faced, you could go to an invisible God and lay your burdens at His feet…or so her parents had said.

God, if You're out there, I beg You to bring my son home alive.

Natalie's chest tightened as pressure built behind her eyes. She bit down on her bottom lip to stem the emotions clawing at her throat.

Setting her mug on the table, she pushed to her feet and reached for her phone.

Mom opened her eyes. "Did you hear something?"

Natalie shook her head. "No, but I can't just sit here. I need to go out and help them look. Maybe I'll call Dad and see where he is and relieve him. It's pouring out there. He must be soaked."

She was referring to her dad, but the thought of Aidan alone, soaked and scared, sent another surge of moisture to her eyes.

The front door slammed open, and Aidan raced in,

soaked to the skin and dripping mud. He carried a black flashlight and motioned for her to follow him. "Mom, come quick. Dad's hurt."

Natalie scooped him up and crushed him to her chest as fresh tears flooded her eyes. "Thank God, you're safe."

He squirmed in her arms until she released him. He reached for her hand and pulled her toward the door. "We have to go. Dad needs us."

"Aidan, hold up." She crouched on the floor in front of him, scanning quickly for injuries. Covered in mud, with his hair plastered to his head and his grimy clothes stuck to his skin, he didn't appear to be harmed. She framed his face with her hands. "What's wrong with your dad?"

"He's at the creek by the bridge. He's hurt. He needed me to be brave and run home. But it was dark. I was scared. But I was brave, Mom. So brave."

She hugged him again. "You sure were."

"Come on, let's go. Dad needs us."

"Not so fast. You're staying here. I've had a big enough scare to last a lifetime. I'll go find your dad." She opened the coat closet on the other side of the front door, pulled out a rain jacket and shoved her feet into her mother's rain boots. "Mom, call Dad and let him know Aidan's been found. I'll call 911 and get help for Evan."

"I wanna go."

"No, Aidan. You need to stay here."

"But I'm brave now, Mom. I'm not scared. And you don't know where to find Dad." The look on her son's face pierced her heart.

"Fine, but we're going to drive and you have to promise to stay in the car."

"I promise." Aidan raced through the kitchen and to the garage where Natalie parked her SUV.

Once he was buckled into his booster seat, Natalie backed out of the garage and headed down the road where she walked the dogs. Tightening her hold on the steering wheel, she bounced along the uneven trail Evan had shown her and Aidan a couple of weeks ago. She drove slowly to the end of the bank.

She could make out the shadow of a vehicle on the other side of the creek. Must be Evan's truck.

She turned in her seat. "Where's your dad?"

"Beside the footbridge." He pointed through the windshield.

"Okay, I'll call for help and be right back. Stay here. Got it?"

"Got it."

After cracking a window for air flow, Natalie shut off the engine but left the headlights on so she could see. Grabbing Aidan's flashlight, she headed for the bank. She shone the light along the creek bed and stopped on Evan's still form, slumped against the bank by the tipped bridge.

Her heart crashed into her ribs. Sitting in the wet grass, she scooted down the side of the bank beside him and cupped his face. "Evan, can you hear me?"

"Nat." His voice was thready. "Aidan. Where's Aidan?"

"Aidan's safe."

"Thank God."

"Yes, thank God. Let's get you out of here." She reached for her phone and called 911. She gave the dispatcher her name, location and her emergency situation.

Time seemed to crawl as she stayed on the line, her attention divided between Evan and Aidan, still in the car.

After what seemed like an eternity, sirens wailed. Emergency lights reflected through the trees as an ambulance drove down the rutted path and parked next to her SUV. Two paramedics decked out in rain gear and carrying emergency kits scaled down the bank next to her.

She moved out the way, bumping into the bridge, and nearly lost her footing. Slowly she climbed up the bank and opened her door to sit in the driver's seat, not ready to leave until she knew Evan was safe.

The rain had slowed to a drizzle.

She heard the crackle of the radio and listened as one of the paramedics requested assistance.

For the second time, Natalie prayed. This time for Evan.

Because she realized without a doubt she couldn't live without him.

Evan just wanted the pain to stop.

He struggled to open his eyes, but his eyelids felt as if they were caked with dried mud.

Images flickered through his head like a silent movie. Tucker and Isabella's wedding. His fight with Natalie. Walking away. Cleaning up with Jake. The news about Aidan.

Aidan.

He had to make sure Aidan was safe.

Evan tried to move, tried to sit up, but he felt pinned.

He forced his eyes open and winced against the light over his bed. He focused on the wall painted a pale green that held a TV and a whiteboard with information. A tug at his right arm showed an IV line had been taped in place. A monitor tracking his vitals beeped when the oximeter slipped off his finger.

His head fell back against the white-cased pillow. He was back in the hospital.

He looked to his left and nearly cried. His left shoulder was wrapped in dressing, which meant only one thing—he'd undergone surgery. His paddling career was toast.

The death of a dream.

Evan dropped his head against his pillow.

What was he going to do now?

Filming the commercial was out. Training for next season was definitely out. He didn't need a specialist to confirm there would be no more seasons for him.

What was in store for a thirty-year-old has-been?

The door to his hospital room opened, and his father walked in, carrying a steaming cup of coffee.

A smile deepened the lines on his face as he pulled a chair closer to Evan's bed. "You're awake. How do you feel?"

"Like I've been tossed around in a cement mixer." His voice sounded hoarse and gravelly.

"That good, huh?"

"Dad, how's Aidan?"

The grin returned. "That brave little boy is doing just fine. He had a thorough checkup. Other than some minor abrasions and bruises, he's in perfect health."

"I hope he's not too traumatized by what happened."

"Ted said he was doing well, but you can call Natalie to double-check."

Evan shook his head. "No, we're done. I'll be polite when it comes to Aidan, but there's no future for Natalie and me. We want different things. She doesn't trust me to keep my word, and I need to be with someone who'll champion my dreams and be my biggest supporter. She has too many fears for us to work."

"Do you love her?"

Evan blew out a breath. "I've been in love with Natalie Bishop since she was eighteen."

"Have you told her?"

"Recently. Yeah, I guess. I mean, I think so. We had an argument at Tuck's wedding reception. I think I said something about loving her then, but my brain feels a little fuzzy right now."

"Sounds like you two need to have another conversation."

Evan scoffed. "The funny thing is she wanted a permanent address. She couldn't be with me when I was competing because she didn't want that lifestyle. I get why, but now there's no way I can go back to competing with my shoulder. So if Nat and I do end up together, how will I know she will be there for me, for my dreams whatever they may be now?"

Dad lifted a shoulder. "It's all a part of trusting each other. If you two want to be together, that's something you will need to hash out."

"Yeah, we'll see." The reality of his situation crashed over him. "What am I going to do, Dad? For the past five years I've been a paddler. I don't know anything else. And now because of this…" He lifted his left shoulder and sucked in a sharp breath when pain flared through the damaged joint. "My career is over."

His father stood and rested a hand on the bed railing by Evan's head. "You're still very young, and you can do anything you want."

"Except paddle."

"Except competitive paddling. But now you're a blank canvas to be used by God for His purpose."

"What can God do with a broken and battered washed-up man?"

"That's the beauty of it—He can do whatever He wants. And He can use you to encourage others."

His father left Evan's bedside, walked over to the corner of the room near a small closet and picked up a magazine from the chair. He leafed through the pages and folded the magazine open. "After the tornado ripped through Holland Hill, we nearly lost everything. Losing your mother crippled me more than the back injury. Claudia's late husband, Dennis, was getting chemo at that time. The man was dying, and he knew it. I was having a fine ol' pity party. He looked me square in the eye and said, 'Chuck, God has just given you a blank canvas with the farm. Rebuild it wisely.' I had no clue what God wanted me to do with it, but I knew He would show me. Several days later, I learned about a program that paired farmers and veterans so they could learn how to build their own small businesses and reestablish that sense of hope and purpose. And I knew God was calling me to do something similar."

"Why haven't I heard this story before?"

"You weren't ready to hear it. You were a cocky water jockey ready to take on the world."

"Not anymore."

"Through the years, your mother and I acquired a lot of property on Holland Hill. You boys had a nice inheritance coming. After Lilly's death, I realized I didn't want you boys to wait until I was gone to have what was yours. Jake had just been discharged from the Marine Corps. After losing his buddy Leo, I knew he needed a project to focus on, so I told him about the farming veterans program and we came up with Fatigues to Farming. That's when I decided to divide up your inheritance with the caveat that a portion needed to be used in some way for the program."

Evan's eyes burned as he struggled to stay awake. "I get how Jake could use part of his property for cabins. And, thanks to Isabella and her dad, Tuck uses his portion for a community garden. But I don't know what I can do."

"Well, you seemed to be doing well with the service dog project, so you could always expand that in some way. Or you may want to consider something like this." Dad handed him the folded-back magazine.

Evan took it and scanned the headline about a veteran without legs who kayaked competitively. That sounded vaguely familiar. Then he searched for the byline and found his own name. "I wrote this."

"Yes, your best article, in my opinion."

Even though his eyes didn't want to focus well, Evan skimmed the paragraphs. "I met Victor last year, and I was so inspired by his story. He'd lost both legs after his Humvee crossed paths with an IED. But he didn't let that stop him from wanting to kayak." Evan looked up at his dad. "He beat me in that race. Did you know that?"

"I didn't. Even though you can't compete anymore, you still have a love of the water. You can set up a project like this to encourage and empower the veterans in our Fatigues to Farming program to do more than they thought possible." Dad sat on the edge of Evan's bed and pressed a hand to his shoulder. "Your identity isn't tied up in being a paddler. You are a child of God and a blank canvas to use as He sees fit. What you may consider the death of a dream may spark hope in someone else. Think about it. Talk to God and allow Him to guide you down a new path. I'm going let you get some sleep, but I'll be back in a bit."

He started to turn, then stopped and pulled something out of his back pocket. "Oh, by the way, we retrieved your phone. Ted went back to get Aidan's backpack and found it on the bank. Pretty smart to have it in a waterproof case. I took it to the wireless shop, and they checked it out. Seems to be working just fine."

"It must've slipped out of my pocket one of the times I fell." Evan took the phone and wrapped his hand around it. "Thanks, Dad."

His father nodded, then walked out the door, closing it quietly behind him.

Evan closed his eyes and sighed.

He had some praying to do. Some choices to make. And an important conversation to have. First, though, he needed sleep.

Chapter Fifteen

Her nightmare had come true.

At least partially.

Missy Chapman sat on one of the red couches in the Bishop living room with a cup of English breakfast tea in her hands. Her shoulder-length red hair fell in beachy waves around her face. With her flawless makeup and polished nails, she advertised the success of her husband's news station. Despite the end-of-August heat, she wore a gray pencil skirt with matching blazer over a soft pink tank and coordinated pumps.

Natalie's parents sat on the couch opposite Missy while Natalie perched on the arm next to her mother, ready to bolt at a moment's notice.

Missy took another sip of tea, then set the cup on the coffee table and crossed her ankles. "As I mentioned to Ted on the phone, our news station loves human interest stories. With everything that's happening in the news right now, people need a breath of fresh air. When we did the piece on the service dog program, we knew it would touch people's hearts, but we never expected it to go viral. Thanks to its spread on social media, it's been picked up by major networks across the country. As a result, we would love to schedule a follow-up to show how the veterans in the Fatigues to Farming program are responding to having service dogs to help them through their daily lives."

Dad leaned forward and rested his elbows on his knees. "You need to be talking with Chuck Holland and his boys. They're the ones spearheading the Fatigues to Farming program."

"Yes, I know, and I plan to, but when we set up the first segment about the service dog project, I understood there were privacy concerns." She looked at Natalie. "I know you didn't want to be a part of the news segment, and then you relented. We did our very best to keep your face off camera, but, Natalie, you were a natural. You really came to life talking about working with the animals. That's why I wanted to come to you first before I approached the Hollands."

They all turned to look at her.

Natalie stood and wrapped her arms around her stomach, trying to do her very best to keep from throwing up in front of their guest.

She assumed what she hoped was a perfectly normal-looking smile. "Thank you for your thoughtful consideration, Missy. I appreciate it. Truly. This is something we will need to discuss as a family. Once we make a decision, we can get back to you."

"Absolutely." Missy stood, brushed invisible wrinkles off the front of her skirt, then reached into her bag and pulled out a business card. She handed it to Natalie. "Feel free to reach me at this number at any time."

After walking her to the door and bidding her goodbye, Natalie returned to the living room, flopped on the spot Missy had just vacated and buried her face in her shaking hands.

Mom sat next to her and placed a hand on her back. "Before you start freaking out, let's remember a couple of things—your face was not shown and it's been twenty years, Natalie."

"I know, Mom. I do. And it's starting to sink into my thick head, but I've carried that fear around me like a security blanket."

"But, honey, a security blanket is a comfort measure. This hasn't brought you comfort. It's fed the fear inside you, limiting what you can do with your life. You've created a wall of protection around yourself, letting very few people in, but also limiting your true potential. You heard Missy—you are a natural when you're working with the dogs. Your skills will be a blessing to someone else."

Dad moved from his spot on the couch and sat on the edge of the coffee table. He took Natalie's hands in his and rubbed his fingers over her knuckles. "Natalie, when you came into my life, I knew you were someone special. I've loved you with my whole heart as if you were my daughter from the day of your birth. But the love I feel for you pales in comparison to how much God loves you. He created you with that beautiful brown hair and those compassionate green eyes. He filled you with gifts and talents that can be used to further His kingdom. Despite what you may think, He has never abandoned you. You say your prayers went unanswered, but I disagree. He answered your prayers by keeping you safe across the country from a man who was no good for you. Your mom gave you a new name, but when you trust God and believe in His promises, He gives you a new identity—daughter."

Her father reached into his back pocket, pulled out his wallet and removed a business card. "This is the name of a local Christian therapist who specializes in post-traumatic stress disorders, even those manifested from childhood trauma like yours. Since you're planning to stay in Shelby Lake, you should see someone closer to home."

Natalie took the card and rubbed her thumb over the embossed lettering. "Thanks, Dad. I'll think about it."

Her mother reached for the business card. "Joanna's mother is a good friend of mine. When I moved back to Shelby Lake, my parents put me in touch with her mother, who is also a therapist, and she helped me learn how to prevent my past from debilitating my future."

Natalie looked up at her mother, whose face radiated serenity. "Is that what you think I'm doing?"

She gave Natalie a gentle smile. "Yes, honey, I do— you've allowed your fears to prevent you from being with the man you love. You're living your life in a bubble, and that's not what God wants for you. You need to continue getting professional help in order to learn how to take control of your thoughts. The Holy Spirit gives us that power. But God also equips others to help us through difficult circumstances."

Hearing the words from her parents threaded with their concern caused the wall inside Natalie to shift.

"I just keep thinking over and over of Aidan and how he kept telling me how brave he was—he was so proud of his actions. He had complete trust in Evan's confidence in him. I realize I've been holding my son back from experiencing things because of my own fears."

Dad gave her hand a little squeeze. "But now you're recognizing that. When you guard your mind against those fearful thoughts and allow your faith to be greater than your fear, you will see how God heals you and grows you to live your best life for Him. That's all we want for you."

"I don't even know where to begin, Dad."

"Punky, that's the easiest part. Just talk to Him. Have a conversation as if He were sitting next to you on the couch. Prayer isn't about perfect words and a pious attitude. It's about meeting Him in the middle of your mess. Trust Him the way Aidan had to trust Evan to save him from the water. Get your brave on and run through the darkness toward home. Then, and only then, will you be able to move past this fear that is keeping you from what you truly want. As you allow God to shelter you in His embrace, He will heal you from the inside out and give you peace from the past."

Peace from the past.

And hope for the future.

Two things she wanted so badly, but before she could have them, she needed to take the first step toward receiving God's grace.

Evan was right back where he'd started.

He had hoped by month's end he'd be preparing to return to the water, but after the difficult conversation with the surgeon, his paddling career was most definitely over.

Without his career, he wouldn't be able to make the payments on the house he'd purchased in order to offer a home for his son when they were together.

And Natalie could use that to keep Evan from being with Aidan.

He sat on the tailgate of his truck and stared at the poured foundation curing in the midafternoon sun. The contractor had arrived as scheduled while Evan was recovering from surgery and couldn't call to change the date.

With a new house coming, more contractor fees for the utility hookups and rising medical bills, the financial burden weighed on Evan's shoulders.

Even if he wrote articles using the hunt-and-peck method with his right hand, he still wouldn't make enough to meet his budget. He'd used most of his savings for the down payment. What was left could keep him going for a month or two, and then he needed to find a job. Something, anything, to help make a dent in the bills that would be rolling in.

His eyes sliced to the Water Wagon. He could sell the RV for a couple of grand.

Man, the thought of doing that caused a burning in his gut.

That would mean shacking up at the farmhouse until his house was finished. As much as he loved his family, he also loved his own space.

But a part of trusting God was leaving all of this in His hands and allowing Him to work it out.

Easier said than done, but he needed to try.

Evan slid off the tailgate, careful not to bump his bandaged arm in the sling, and whistled for River and Toby, who were sniffing around the foundation.

Their ears perked, and they raced over to the truck.

Evan lifted a finger and they sat, their eyes on him.

"Good boys." Evan rubbed their heads, pulled a treat

from his pocket, broke it in half with one hand and fed a piece to each of them. "Want to head back to the farm?"

He opened the passenger-side door for them to jump into the back seat. A car crested the hill and pulled in next to his truck.

He rounded the front as Natalie stepped out of her SUV, wearing the same pink *LOVE* shirt she'd worn the day he'd returned to Shelby Lake. Her gorgeous hair fell around her shoulders and he wanted nothing more than to run his fingers through it. She moved to the back of her SUV, opened the back hatch and lifted out a piece of fencing.

After closing the hatch, she returned to where he was standing. She rested the fencing against her car, slid her sunglasses onto her head and gave him a timid smile. "Hi."

"Hey, Nat."

"How are you feeling?"

He shrugged. "Fine."

She looked over his shoulder at the foundation, then directed her attention back to him. "Can we talk?"

"Sure. What do you want to talk about?"

"First and most importantly, I wanted to thank you for saving Aidan. That was the scariest night of my life." Her eyes brightened with unshed tears. She dropped her gaze to her feet, then looked at him again. "When he burst through the door, it was an answer to prayer. Then he was so insistent about finding you. He kept telling me over and over how brave he was."

Evan smiled. "He's one courageous little dude."

"He's been asking about you. Wants to see you."

"Yeah, well, I've been pretty out of it for a few days."

She nodded. "I know. I'm so sorry about your shoulder."

Shaking his head, he scoffed. "Your wish came true. My career is over. I won't be returning to the water. I'm staying put in Shelby Lake."

She lowered her gaze again. "I'm sorry. Believe me, Evan, that's not what I wanted for you."

"What *do* you want for me, Nat? Seems to me, you want me on your terms, but I can't live like that."

She shook her head. "No, I don't want that, either. Missy Chapman visited us this morning and said the service dog clip had gone viral and was being picked up by major news networks across the country."

"Oh, wow, Nat, I'm sorry. That's the total opposite of what you wanted."

She nodded. "Yes, I know. After she left, I was on the verge of a panic attack and had a very long talk with my parents. I have a lot of fears, Evan. You may have noticed."

He grinned. "Just a little."

Natalie dragged her hand through her hair, knocking her glasses off her head. She reached down to pick them up off the ground and tossed them on the front seat of her car. "I've put up walls—for personal protection—but as I learned over the past few days, those walls will not keep my son safe. In fact, my fears caused Aidan to run away. Once we returned from getting him checked out at the hospital, he confessed to overhearing part of my conversation with my mom. After you and I had argued at the wedding, I told my mom I wanted to take Aidan and run."

Evan's muscles tightened.

Natalie held up a hand. "Relax. It was just my fear

talking. Mom talked me off the ledge, but by then it was too late—Aidan had left. So while I thought I was protecting my son, I was putting him in jeopardy. I'm so sorry, Evan. I hope you can forgive me." A tear drifted down her face. She brushed it away. "Anyway, I've realized the walls are shutting out the people I love most."

She turned and reached for the piece of fencing. "I brought you a housewarming gift."

"Don't people usually wait until the house is in place for something like that?"

She shrugged. "Apparently, I'm not most people." She slid her hand across the top slat. "This is the gate piece that attaches to vinyl fencing. A gate is surrounded by walls, but it opens to allow others to enter. I'm meeting with a new therapist on Monday to learn how to break down those walls. In the meantime, I'm giving this gate to you and inviting you into my life." She smiled through a sheen of tears. "I love you, Evan. And I will do whatever it takes and go where you want to go if it means we can be together as a family."

The words he'd been waiting so long to hear should have had him reaching out for her and pulling her to his chest. Yet, he didn't move. He couldn't.

He dragged a hand through his hair. "Nat…"

"I'm too late, aren't I?" She dropped her gaze to her feet.

"No, it's not that. More than anything I want to accept the gift you're offering, but I can't."

"Why not?"

"Because…" He turned away from her as pressure mounted in his chest. "I have nothing to offer you."

She looked at him with a crease in her forehead. "What do you mean?"

He waved a hand over his arm. "My career is over. I live in an RV. I have to figure out how to pay for a house that I can no longer afford. And I have my own fears. After this past week, the last place I want to be is on the water. Imagine that—a paddler afraid of the water."

He drew in a deep breath and let it out slowly. He reached out for her, but instead of touching her, he dropped his hand.

"All I have is my heart." His voice cracked on the last word.

A slow smile lit up her face. "Out of all those things you've mentioned, that's the only thing I'm after."

"Really?"

"Yes, Evan, really. Your life is a mess. Guess what? So is mine. But if we keep God in center of our messy lives, then we will do just fine."

He searched her face, looking for a hint of sarcasm, but all he found were her beautiful bottle-green eyes filled with love and sincerity. He reached for her, lifting his hand through her hair and pulling her close. "I love you, Natalie. I don't know what the future holds and I can't promise what kind of security I can offer you, but as long as you and Aidan are a part of it, I know it will be perfect."

"I love you, too, Evan. God will provide us with the security we need."

"I'm so grateful to hear you say that." Evan cupped Nat's cheek and caressed his thumb over her cheekbone. He lowered his head and brushed his lips over hers.

Who could have predicted that losing everything would give him exactly what he'd always wanted?

Epilogue

Who knew the year would end like this?

With a steaming mug of hot chocolate in her mittened hands, Natalie stood on the back deck of Evan's beautiful home, stamping her booted feet together to generate heat, and watched as father and son built a snowman together.

Tall evergreens and leafless branches behind them wore heavy blankets of snow, turning the otherwise bare limbs into a winter wonderland. A light wind swirled snow around the duo as flurries dusted their reddened cheeks.

Dressed in his royal blue snow pants and matching jacket with a red Spider-Man hat on his head, Aidan rolled the last ball and allowed Evan to lift it up to put on the snowman's shoulders. Then he thrust his arms in the air and called out to her. "Look, Mom, we did it. We made a snow family. One for each of us."

"You sure did." Natalie pulled off her mitten with her teeth and reached into her back pocket for her phone. She snapped a picture of them in front of the trio of snow people. "You guys ready for hot chocolate yet?"

Evan waved an arm for her to join them. "Come on down and we'll get a picture of all of us with our snow family."

She stowed her phone, tugged her mitten back on and wrapped her favorite blue scarf around her neck. She'd be fine in her red sweater and white down vest for a few minutes. She hurried down the deck steps to the backyard and posed next to Aidan in front of their newly built snow family. Evan moved in next to her, pulled out his phone and stretched out his long arms to snap the selfie.

Natalie rubbed her hands over her arms and stamped her feet together. "It's freezing out here. Let's head inside and get warm before we head down to the farm for the New Year's Eve party."

Evan unzipped his coat and shrugged it off his shoulders. He wrapped it around Natalie. "In just a minute. I need to ask Aidan something."

Natalie gave him a quizzical look, but he just smiled.

He turned to Aidan and hunkered down on one knee front of him. "Hey, A-man, how would you like it if you, your mom and I lived in the same house forever and ever?"

Aidan's eyes widened, and then he threw his arms around Evan's neck. "Yes! I would really love that!"

A gasp caught in her throat as her heart hammered against her rib cage.

Did he…

Shifting Aidan to his left side, Evan turned to Natalie, reached into his front jeans pocket and pulled out a delicate silver ring that glimmered in the moonlight. "These past four months with you and Aidan have showed me exactly what I want in my life—to be together as a family under one roof. I love you, Natalie Grace—will you marry me?"

Laughing through a blur of tears, she nodded. "Yes, Evan, I will."

He slid the ring onto her finger. "My dad gave this opal ring to my mom on the day I was born. I know it's not a traditional engagement ring, but let's face it—we're not exactly the most traditional family. If you'd prefer a diamond or something else, say the word and it's yours."

She held up her hand to admire the iridescent stone sparkling from the delicate setting, and she shook her head. "No way. This one's perfect."

She pulled Evan to his feet, curled her arms around his neck and feathered a kiss across his lips.

"Gross. Kissy kind of love." Aidan stuck out his tongue.

Evan laughed, the rich timbre of his voice warming her from the inside out. "That's right, pal. Get used to it."

He pressed his forehead against Natalie's. "I promise to love you until I take my last breath. Thank you for being my champion these past few months. I know it's been tough as we've been working hard to get the River Therapy project off the ground, but when spring hits, we'll be ready."

She cupped her hand over his cold cheek. "Thank you for standing by me as I work through my fears. And for not laughing at me when I became a fostering failure by not being able to give up Daisy."

Evan dropped a kiss on the end of her nose. "You're so tenderhearted, Nat. While I will support you in every way throughout this program, we now know you don't make a good foster dog mom."

"It's hard to say goodbye."

He brought her hands to her lips and brushed a kiss across her knuckles. "And soon, we won't have to say good-night and go our separate ways."

"When would you like to get married?"

"Is tomorrow too soon?"

"It would be the perfect way to begin the New Year, but let's do it right."

"Hey, you two. Your hot chocolate's getting cold." Aidan waved to them from the glass sliding door that led into the open kitchen.

Hand in hand, they walked across the backyard and up the deck steps. Natalie stepped into the warmth of the kitchen, but Evan stopped. He flung his arms out wide and took a deep breath.

"What are you doing?"

"The air is so fresh. It's like breathing in God's grace—it cleanses from the inside out."

And breathing in God's grace had given her all the peace and security she needed to find what her heart truly wanted. A family to call her own and the father her son deserved.

* * * * *

If you loved this story,
pick up Lisa Jordan's
previous books set in Shelby Lake:

Lakeside Sweethearts
Lakeside Redemption
Lakeside Romance
Season of Hope
A Love Redeemed

Available now from Love Inspired!

Find more great reads at LoveInspired.com.

Dear Reader,

Several years ago, I bought a canvas with the verse Joshua 1:9 printed on it. It hangs by my front door, and each time I leave, I'm reminded God is with me wherever I go.

I'm not necessarily a strong person. But in the last decade or so, I've had to learn how to trust God and step out of my comfort zone in order to live my best life—a life in the center of His will. As someone who internalizes fears and anxieties, it hasn't been easy, but God's faithfulness helps to grow my strength, my courage and, yes, my faith. Throughout my life, I've missed out on blessings because of my fears. But I'm learning how to be brave and to embrace His grace when I'm not feeling very strong or courageous.

When I wrote Evan and Natalie's story, I wanted to write about characters who struggle with fear and anxiety. Evan has nonmilitary PTSD after a traumatic accident that nearly killed him. Natalie struggled with childhood trauma. But through their faith in God, they are learning how to overcome their fears. One day at a time.

If you, my dear readers, struggle with fears and anxiety, please know you are not alone. And remember God is with you wherever you go. He provides resources to help you—trained counselors, medications, support groups and books written by others who have walked the same road. I encourage you to seek help if your fear and anxiety stand in the way of you living your best life. Mental illness is a medical condition that deserves to be recognized and treated without being stigmatized.

Stay strong, warriors, even on days when you don't feel brave or courageous, because God sees you, and He's with you every step of the way. Allow Him to use you for His glory.

I love to hear from my readers, so feel free to email me at lisa@lisajordanbooks.com.

Embracing His grace,
Lisa Jordan

COURTING HIS AMISH WIFE
by Emma Miller

When Levi Miller learns Eve Summy is about to be forced to marry her would-be attacker or risk being shunned, he marries her instead. Now husband and wife, but complete strangers, the two have to figure out how to live together in harmony...and maybe even find love along the way.

HER PATH TO REDEMPTION
by Patrice Lewis

Returning to the Amish community she left during her *rumspringa*, widowed mother Eliza Struder's determined to redeem the wild reputation of her youth. But one woman stands between her and acceptance into the church—the mother of the man she left behind. Can she convince the community—and Josiah Lapp—to give her a second chance?

THE COWGIRL'S SACRIFICE
Hearts of Oklahoma • by Tina Radcliffe

Needing time to heal after a rodeo injury, Kate Rainbolt heads to her family ranch to accept the foreman job her brothers offered her months ago. But the position's already been filled by her ex-boyfriend, Jess McNally. With Jess as her boss—and turning into something more—this wandering cowgirl might finally put down roots...

A FUTURE TO FIGHT FOR
Bliss, Texas • by Mindy Obenhaus

Single father Crockett Devereaux and widow Paisley Wainwright can't get through a church-committee meeting without arguing—and now they have to work together to turn a local castle into a museum and wedding venue. But first they must put their differences aside...and realize they make the perfect team.

THE MISSIONARY'S PURPOSE
Small Town Sisterhood • by Kat Brookes

Wounded and back home after a mission trip, Jake Landers never expected his estranged friend Addy Mitchell to offer help. She hurt him by keeping secrets, and he's not sure he can trust her. But when their friendship sparks into love, can he forgive her...and give her his heart?

FINDING HER COURAGE
by Christine Raymond

Inheriting part of a ranch is an answer to prayers for struggling widow Camille Bellamy and her little girl—except Ty Spencer was left the rest of it. They strike a bargain: he'll agree to sell the ranch if she helps plan an event that could keep his business afloat. But can their arrangement stay strictly professional?

_____

LOOK FOR THESE AND OTHER LOVE INSPIRED BOOKS WHEREVER BOOKS ARE SOLD, INCLUDING MOST BOOKSTORES, SUPERMARKETS, DISCOUNT STORES AND DRUGSTORES.

LICNM0721

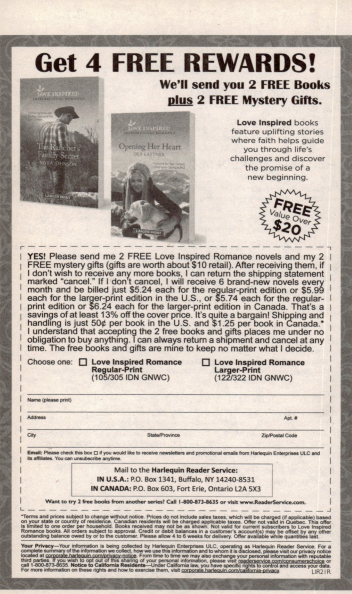